THE DRAGON DETECTIVE AGENCY

THE CASE OF THE WAYWARD PROFESSOR

By the same author

The Dragon Detective Agency:
The Case of the Missing Cats

THE DRAGON DETECTIVE AGENCY

THE CASE OF THE WAYWARD PROFESSOR

GARETH P. JONES

BLOOMSBURY

First published in Great Britain in 2007 by Bloomsbury Publishing Plc,
36 Soho Square, London, W1D 3QY

Text copyright © 2007 by Gareth P. Jones
Illustrations copyright © 2007 by Nick Price

A CIP catalogue record of this book is available from the British Library

ISBN 978 0 7475 8624 1

Printed and bound in Great Britain by Clays Ltd, St Ives Plc

3 5 7 9 10 8 6 4 2

All papers used by Bloomsbury Publishing are natural, recyclable products made from
wood grown in well-managed forests. The manufacturing processes conform
to the environmental regulations of the country of origin.

To Lesley and Leslie
(AKA Mum and Dad)
– G.J.

Chapter One

Holly stopped by the door and, for a fleeting moment, considered making a run for it there and then. The electronic whirring of a security camera brought her to her senses, its automated sensor detecting her movement. This was not the time. *Remember the plan.* Holly looked up at the lens, stuck her tongue out at it and continued down the corridor to the principal's office.

The escape would be tonight, but it wasn't going to be easy. William Scrivener School prided itself on being as inescapable as it was impenetrable. Every corridor was watched by state-of-the-art CCTV cameras, monitored round the clock by a private security service. The best time for an escape was at night when there were two guards on duty rather than three and it was easier to hide from the cameras. The problem with a night escape was the external doors which were opened using coded electronic wristbands. All pupils were issued with non-removable green wristbands but these were programmed only to open the doors during the day, unlike the teachers' red wristbands that worked round the clock.

But even if you got past the cameras, avoided being seen by the teachers who patrolled the corridors, and somehow got through the door, you still had to make it across the school grounds, without being picked up by security or smelt by the guard dogs, and find a way over, under or through the high wire fence that surrounded the school.

Then you were free to begin the ten-mile walk through the large forest to the nearest village, the aptly named Little Hope.

As the school of choice for the ridiculously rich and phenomenally famous, William Scrivener's security was the most intense Holly had ever encountered, but getting out of school was what Holly did best.

She arrived at the principal's office and approached the desk where a large woman with carrot-red hair and blue eyeliner was painting her nails purple. Without looking up, she pressed a half-painted nail on the intercom button. 'Holly Bigsby is here for your daily meeting, Principal Palmer,' she said, her voice rich with sarcasm.

'Send her in, Angie,' replied the principal.

Holly entered the dark wood office. In the twenty-seven days she had been at the school this was her twenty-eighth visit to the principal's office, but it was the first time she had got herself sent there on purpose.

'Morning, Holly,' said the principal, adjusting his tie in the reflection of one of the many shiny awards that stood on the mantelpiece.

'Hello, sir,' replied Holly, glancing at the desk where his red wristband lay. On her previous visits she had noticed that, unlike her wristband, the principal's was removable and that he took it off on Fridays so that it didn't clash with his navy blue suit.

'What is it today, disruptive behaviour or insolence?' he asked, a tanned hand neatening his hair.

'Speaking out of turn, sir.'

'Ah.' Principal Palmer nodded understandingly. 'What happened?'

'Miss Whittaker told us about *When Petals Blossom* being on the syllabus.'

'Yes. Terrific news, isn't it? Our stock has gone up three points.'

Holly said nothing.

'It's had a lot of press coverage.' The principal grabbed a newspaper off a pile on his desk and read it out. 'Having already written her autobiography at the tender age of eleven, now pop's most famous offspring, Petal Moses will be studying it at school . . .'

Holly edged nearer to the desk, keeping her eyes fixed on the principal.

'. . . after it was selected for the English curriculum.'

Holly reached out towards the wristband.

'Described by one critic as "a deeply insightful account of what it means to grow up in the full glare of the harsh media spotlight," the book will be studied by year seven students across the country, including Petal herself.'

The principal chuckled at this and looked up. Holly quickly lowered her hand.

He smiled and continued. '"Petal Moses is one of our most talented students, and that's saying something," said Larry Palmer, the self-titled Principal of William Scrivener School."' He beamed at Holly, and placed the paper back on his desk.

Holly needed that wristband.

'Could you read me another one?' she asked.

Principal Palmer raised an eyebrow in surprise. 'Yes, of course,' he said, picking up another paper and reading: '"Studying her own autobiography won't be an unfair advantage for precocious Petal Moses . . ."'

Holly's hand neared the wristband.

'". . . because most critics agree that spoilt pop brat Petal didn't actually write it . . ."'

The principal slammed the paper down and Holly whipped her hand away again.

'Yes, well, there's always some degree of negativity from the cynics,' he said. 'Petal's your room-mate, isn't she? Aren't you pleased for her?'

Holly scowled. Petal Moses was pleased enough for herself. To say that Petal had got everything she had ever wanted was an understatement. She had got much more than that. If she wanted a new party dress, she was flown out by private helicopter to an exclusive department store, where a personal shopper awaited. If she liked a new pop band, they would be brought to the school for a private performance, which only she and her friends could attend. Even some of the teachers pandered to her. Miss Whittaker, their English teacher, had been beside herself when she announced that they would be studying her book, and Petal's fawning friends had burst into applause.

'What happened when Miss Whittaker told you?' asked the principal.

'I said that I thought the title was stupid because petals don't blossom. I said that flowers blossom. Petals just fall off and die.'

'I see, and you said this in front of the whole class, did you?'

'Yes.'

'Now, Holly, you really must try to make an effort to fit in. William Scrivener is the finest school in the country. Your parents were very lucky to get you in at all. And you should feel honoured to be sharing a room with a student as special as Petal.'

'Special?' said Holly. 'There's nothing special about her?'

Principal Palmer sighed. 'I know that your father is important, too. MPs are important people, even back-benchers.'

'He's not a backbencher. Dad works in the Ministry of Defence,' Holly interrupted. 'He might make the Cabinet this year.'

'Very impressive, I'm sure,' he replied. 'But Petal's mother is known all round the world.' The principal clapped his hands together and, as though it was the highest compliment anyone could ever be paid, added, 'And she's American.'

'Well, I hate her, and I hate this stupid school,' Holly shouted, lashing out and knocking the pile of newspapers to the floor.

'Holly Bigsby!' barked the principal, diving to pick them up.

Holly seized the opportunity, snatched the wristband and thrust it into her pocket.

The principal placed the papers back on to the table, careful not to crease them.

'I don't know what's wrong with you,' he said sternly, 'but if you think you can get expelled from this school, you can think again. Your parents have paid a lot of money to keep you here.'

This was Holly's sixth school. She was taken out of her last one after only one term when her dad's big-haired wife had decided to send her away. The general election had been called and she didn't want Holly's bad behaviour attracting any negative press attention. Dad hadn't phoned since she had been there, but she guessed he was busy with the campaign.

'Yes, sir, sorry, sir,' said Holly, her voice full of fake remorse.

He smiled kindly and tilted his head. 'You know, this

school can open many doors in life, but only if you let it. Why don't you make some friends?'

Holly didn't want any of these people as friends. They were all the same, spoilt rich kids who rode their ponies on Saturdays and argued over who lived in the biggest house, or whose parents were the most famous.

The only real friend she had made was Little Willow, but she didn't admit to this because Little Willow was a mouse and she didn't want Principal Palmer to think she was a nutcase. She had found her under the bed when she first arrived in her dorm and named her after her cat, Willow, whom she had left behind with a private detective she knew, called Dirk Dilly.

She missed Willow.

She missed Dirk too. She had written to him twice a week since being at the school, but he hadn't replied. She would have phoned but Petal had told her that all outgoing calls were recorded because of the school's paranoia that students might sell stories about each other to the press. Holly couldn't risk them finding out about Dirk. He wasn't just a friend. He wasn't just a private detective. Dirk Dilly was a real genuine, fire-breathing dragon.

Chapter Two

If the commuters had taken a moment to stop, they might have seen two yellow lights flicker on the sloping roof of the bank opposite the station. If they had looked up they might have noticed that the lights were actually two eyes, and that the flicker was, in fact, a blink. If they had peered very carefully, they would have realised that the eyes belonged to the dragon-shaped lump perfectly camouflaged against the rooftop.

But this was Moorgate, the business district of London, and it was a grey rainy Friday morning. No one stopped, or looked up, or paid the slightest bit of attention to the dragon watching them. They traipsed out of the tube station hurrying to get out of the drizzle into their warm, dry offices, where they could sit down, make a cup of coffee and while away the day staring at their computer screens, counting the hours until they could go home again.

Dirk Dilly's yellow eyes focused on a man in a grey suit, struggling to open an umbrella without dropping his briefcase. A gust of wind caught the umbrella, blowing it inside out. The man cursed and threw it in a bin. The drizzle became rain and landed on the hairless top of his head, running down to the top of his clumps of grey hair that sprouted around his ears and the top of his neck.

He took a right turn down a narrow lane and Dirk sprang into action, his back reverting to its usual red as he flew, spreading his wings and gliding down to another roof. He had to be careful in this part of the city, where bored workers might easily glance down from their tall office blocks and see him.

The consequences of being seen were unthinkable, which was why most dragons avoided cities, preferring to hide in more remote corners of the globe – the bottom of the deepest oceans, the top of the highest mountains, or far down in the belly of the earth itself.

Many years ago, the Dragon Council realised that it would be impossible to share the world with the race of strange bipedal mammals that called itself mankind. A conference was called high in the Himalayas. All of dragonkind voted on whether to annihilate humans before they created weapons so powerful as to make them impossible to destroy, or whether to go into hiding until mankind went the way of the dinosaurs. The dragons in favour of fighting rose into the air, while those who wanted to hide stayed on the ground, and it was decided by majority vote that mankind would be allowed to run its course. Attacking humans, being seen by a human, or allowing a human to find any evidence of dragon existence were all made punishable by banishment to the earth's Inner Core.

But Dirk was quick and experienced and, like all Mountain Dragons, whenever he was at rest he could blend his skin to match the surface beneath. It was a useful skill in this busy part of the city. Dirk's work had brought him here many times before, following cheating husbands who told their wives they were working late, or taking pictures of disgruntled employees conducting secret meetings with rival companies. London was full of corruption and deception and Dirk had seen it all.

The man turned down an alleyway. Dirk jumped again, grabbed on to a flagpole that stuck out of the side of a building, swung round twice, catapulting himself into the air and down on to the next building, where he stopped dead. The alleyway led on to another road, where the man entered a large glass-fronted building. He greeted the security guard and took the lift to the sixth floor, where he hung up his coat and settled down at his desk.

Dirk settled too, blending with the office roof, and preparing for another dull day's detective work. This wasn't the most exciting case in the world, but business had been quiet since his last big job, when he had been hired to find a missing cat in South London and ended up foiling the plans of a band of rebel dragons, known as the Kinghorns, intent on destroying mankind. He had also found the cat.

Since then, he had looked out for any dragons in the human world or any signs of what their mysterious leader, Vainclaw Grandin, might be planning next, but hunting Kinghorns wasn't going to pay the rent and he was getting tired of hiding from Mrs Klingerflim, his landlady.

He had received the call five days ago. Dirk conducted all his business over the phone.

'The Dragon Detective Agency,' he said, 'Dirk Dilly speaking.'

'Oh, hello, yes, I need your help,' a female voice replied nervously.

'What can I do for you, madam?' he asked, his feet on the desk, watching Willow jumping up, trying to catch the smoke mice he had been blowing, looking perplexed each time one vanished beneath her paw. Never learning. *Stupid animal*, thought Dirk, stroking her with his tail and wondering why Holly still hadn't been in contact. Maybe she was enjoying her new school and making some human friends for a change.

'My husband has been acting suspiciously,' said the woman. 'I know his work is important to him but he's become increasingly secretive, he gets strange phone calls and comes home and locks himself in his study every night.' She sounded tearful. 'I feel like I'm losing him.'

'OK,' said Dirk. 'I'll find out what he's up to, but are you sure you want to know? In my experience secretive husbands are very rarely organising surprise parties for their wives.'

'I need to know,' she said, 'before it's too late.'

Dirk took down the details.

Professor Karl Rosenfield
Scientist for a company called NAPOW

Fast forward four days and Dirk had never followed anyone less suspicious. Every day was the same. He kissed his wife goodbye and walked to the station. He always bought a copy of the *Telegraph* from the newsagent in the station, picking up the newspaper in his right hand and handing over the correct change with his left. He caught the 8:11 train to Liverpool Street, travelled one tube stop to Moorgate, where he exited and walked to work. He took the same route every day, spoke to the same security guard for the same amount of time, took the same lift to the same floor, hung his same coat in the same place and sat at the same desk until lunchtime, when he bought the same sandwich (ham and pickle on brown) from the same sandwich shop.

At half past five every day he did the whole journey in reverse, reaching home at between 18:24 on a good day and 18:38 on a bad one. After dinner, he went upstairs to his study while his wife watched soaps on her own in the living room. He kept a blue roller blind pulled down in the study window, so Dirk couldn't see inside.

Today was Friday and Dirk was expecting the same, so it came as a surprise when at half past five instead of grabbing his coat, the professor remained at his desk, staying there another hour until everyone had left the building and the sun had gone down, then slipping out of a side door. Instead of his usual briefcase, he carried a large silver case, and rather than walking to the station he hailed a black cab.

The sky was dark, the air, cold and moist. Dirk moved to the edge of the building, spread his wings and glided to the next rooftop, landing into a forward roll then springing up again. He followed the taxi to the outskirts of the financial district, where the buildings looked older and grubbier. It stopped by a disused red-brick hospital, which had worn brickwork and smashed and boarded-up windows. Dirk landed on the roof and peered over the edge.

Professor Rosenfield paid the taxi driver and watched him drive away. A man at the other end of the road was selling watermelons outside a nearby mosque. Rosenfield glanced round then slipped inside the old hospital.

Dirk found a door on the roof, shouldered it open and entered, pulling it shut with his tail and following a flight of stairs down.

He moved quickly and silently through the gloomy building, stealthily slipping down the corridors, listening for footsteps. Dirk wasn't easily scared but there was something spooky about the old, dark and deserted hospital corridors.

He heard the professor's voice coming from the floor below.

'Hello?' he said. 'Is there anyone here?'

Dirk noticed a light coming from a hole in the floor. He crouched down and put his eye to it. He could see Professor Rosenfield enter what looked like an old operating theatre, carrying a torch. He looked nervous.

'Hello?' said Rosenfield again. 'Are you . . . Are you there?'

'Do not come any further,' said a deep baritone voice. Dirk couldn't see who it belonged to.

'I can't see you,' said the professor.

'That's the idea,' replied the voice. 'Is that it?'

'Oh yes, yes. This is it.' He held up the silver case.

'And you are sure no one suspects anything?'

'Positive. The AOG project is top secret, but I can't see what use it is to you. I told you, I can enter coordinates, but you can't operate it without . . .'

The deep voice interrupted him. 'This is not your concern, professor.'

'What about your side of the bargain?' asked the professor.

'It's in the parcel,' said the gravelly voice.

The professor walked to the middle of the room, where he picked up a brown parcel.

'Open it,' said the voice.

The professor did so excitedly like a child opening a Christmas present. Dirk couldn't see what was inside, but he saw the professor's face light up and a tear form in the corner of his eye. 'My goodness,' he gasped. 'Is it real?'

'Yes, and there'll be more once you have reprogrammed the machine. The coordinates are also in there.'

The professor looked up vacantly then blinked and said, 'This is very marvellous.'

'Thank you, Professor Rosenfield. Now go home and I will contact you shortly with details of where you should go next,' said the voice. 'Please make sure that no one knows of this.'

'Gosh, no.'

Rosenfield tucked the parcel under his arm, picked up the silver case and left the room.

Dirk kept his eye on the room below, wanting to catch a glimpse of the owner of the deep voice. He shifted slightly to get a better view, waiting for him to step into sight, but no one appeared. He heard a noise and raised his head, but not quickly enough. A sharp pain shot through his skull and he slumped on the ground, knocked unconscious.

Chapter Three

Holly could hear Petal's voice from the other end of the girls' dormitory corridor.

'I don't give two hoots how much they love the book. It isn't enough money and no one else can play me. I don't care how many Oscars she's got. I'll play myself.'

Holly entered the room. Petal, her thin blonde hair pulled back into a ponytail, wearing a T-shirt with the cover of her mum's latest album on the front, was pacing with her mobile phone held to her ear.

'Just tell them or I'll go with the Disney offer and please stop back-chatting me.' She switched off the phone, exclaimed, 'Agents!' and threw herself on to her bed.

She looked up at Holly. 'Oh, hi there,' she said frostily.

'Hello, Petal,' replied Holly.

'Look, I don't want there to be any bad feelings between us. I understand why you said what you did in class and I forgive you. I know you're jealous of me.'

'I'm not jealous of you,' replied Holly.

'It's totally understandable. I'd be jealous of me if I wasn't me. I called Hermann. He's my therapist and he explained the whole thing. I actually feel sorry for you now,' said Petal, forcing her face into an unnatural-looking smile.

A few days ago a comment like that would have caused Holly to blow up into a raging ball of indignation, but today she bit her lip. Today she could rise above anything Petal threw at her. Today she was getting out.

'Sure,' she said calmly. 'Thanks.'

'And I've looked into it. Bob says the title isn't supposed to be taken literally. It's figurative.'

Bob was the man Petal had employed to write the book for her.

'And you can thank me,' Petal continued, 'I've sorted out the pest problem.'

Holly felt the colour drain from her face. 'What?' she said.

Petal lifted up the duvet to reveal, under the bed, a mousetrap with a dead mouse caught in it, its neck broken in two. 'I've asked the caretaker to come and remove it,' she said, looking pleased with herself.

Holly clapped her hand to her mouth to stop herself screaming.

It was Little Willow.

Murdered.

Late that night Holly lay in bed, fully clothed beneath the sheets; her trainers, coat and bag by the door.

She didn't want Petal to know how much Little Willow had meant to her, so had said nothing and waited until she left the room before taking out the dead mouse and burying her in the school grounds, with a solemn vow to avenge her death.

'No, Mummy,' muttered Petal in her sleep. 'It has to be real fur.'

Holly listened as footsteps passed outside the door. The overnight teacher patrolled every hour. Once they had gone, she checked her watch. It had just gone midnight. Time to go. She pulled back the covers, slipped out of bed, crept across the room and picked up her things. She pulled open the door and stepped out.

Still in her socks, she darted across to a cupboard and climbed in. This was a blind spot. No cameras. She put on her trainers, her black coat over her black jumper and the black balaclava she had fashioned from a bobble hat by cutting out eye holes and pulling it over her face. She slipped her bag over her shoulder and emerged.

Sticking to the shadows, hoping that no one would be staring too intently at the cameras at this time of night, she made her way to the exit. She pulled out the principal's wristband and held it up to the door. A red light turned green and the door buzzed open.

She slid out and dived behind one of the large shrubs that stood on either side of the doorway. The door clicked shut behind her. From what she had learned about the security cabin she knew that a light would be blinking on the console inside, indicating that the door had been opened. One of the guards would be examining all monitors covering that area, checking for any unusual activity. Seeing nothing, they would hopefully assume it was just one of the prefects nipping back after a crafty smoke.

It was a cold night. She was wearing her warmest jumper and jeans, but her ankles were exposed. She needed to get moving to warm up. She waited another minute, counting the seconds on her watch, checked that no one was coming and then moved.

The concrete courtyard between the buildings and the playing fields offered no cover. Holly's only option was to make a run for it. If she had her timings right, the night guard would be way over on the other side of the building. As for the guard in the security cabin, having only just checked the cameras around the girls' dorm, he would hopefully be watching the football game that had just started on TV.

She ran across the courtyard. It seemed a lot further tonight than on the practice runs and her footsteps sounded like someone clapping in a large empty hall. Reaching the playing field, she took cover behind the first of the tall conifer trees that lined the private road which ran from the main buildings to the perimeter gate.

She climbed high into the tree until she was hidden in the darkness of its dense leaves. She remained still for a moment, listened, then climbed along a thick branch to the next tree. She had practised the route several times but her previous attempts had all been made with the benefit of daylight. It was proving more difficult at night. She had a torch but it would have been suicide to turn it on. Her foot slipped and she grabbed a branch to avoid falling, thinking perhaps it was suicide not to use it.

She hung silently in the tree for a second, the rough bark digging into her hand, suddenly aware of the sound of her own breathing. The trees rustled loudly in the breeze. She thought she heard someone cough. She listened. No, it must have been her imagination. There was no one there.

Slowly she made her way from tree to tree until she reached the last one, just far enough from the high wire fence to make a jump impossible. She climbed down to the lowest branch then dropped to the ground, landing badly on her ankle. It hurt and she wanted to shout in pain but kept quiet. The security cabin was only twenty metres away. She could see the light on inside.

Using the trees as cover, she ran along the fence to a point just out of sight of the cameras. She took her bag off her shoulder and pulled out a pair of large wire cutters that she had lifted from her technical design class. One thing you could say about William Scrivener, it was well supplied. Only the best for the children of the best.

She lifted the cutters up to the wire and was about to cut when she felt a hand land on her shoulder and pull her sharply away from the fence.

'All right, far enough,' said a girl's voice.

She felt the wire cutters being pulled away from her other hand. 'Let me go,' she cried, turning round.

'Why, so you can escape?'

Holly recognised the older black girl as one of the prefects.

The girl smiled and said, 'Don't be too annoyed. You got a lot further than I did on my first run.'

Chapter Four

Dirk opened his eyes, raised his head and groaned. He was still in the old hospital, exactly where he had fallen. The room was empty. The light in the room below had gone out. His head pounded.

He crept to the window and looked out. Yellow street light illuminated the melon man, who was packing away. *I can't have been out long*, Dirk thought, *but long enough to lose the professor.*

Checking the room for clues, he found a plank of wood. He examined it. White paint and nail holes indicated that it had once been a shelf. He could see where it had been ripped from the wall. The shelf was broken in the middle where the wood had splintered and the paint fallen away. He touched the top of his head and inspected his paw. Flecks of white paint. This was what knocked him out. On the other end of the shelf was a semicircle of holes. There was no mistaking them. Dragon tooth marks. This was bad news. Once again, it meant that Dirk wasn't the only dragon in London.

Every type of dragon was different. Not just in colour, but in shape, strength, powers, and jaw shape. A grey-backed, blue-bellied Sea Dragon, for example, had a pointy nose, enabling it to cut through the water at great speed, while a Tree Dragon's teeth were longer and sharp enough to cull the mightiest oak.

The jaw that had torn the shelf from the wall had left a more rounded imprint and belonged to a Shade-Hugger, an earth-dwelling dragon that couldn't bear sunlight and only ever surfaced at night, if then. It had been dark when he had arrived at the hospital, so the Shade-Hugger that had knocked him out had probably been there before he arrived. Dirk knew of only one local Shade-Hugger.

'Karnataka,' he growled, running up the stairs to the roof. The air was cold and sharp. He took a moment to consider his route then leapt to the next building, then the next, heading south to the river, able to move quickly with darkness as his cover.

He darted up a block of flats, built like a giant staircase in the sky, and looked down. By the river, in a small park next to a children's playground, was a large cylindrical red-stone building. To the locals who used the park it was an air vent for one of the car tunnels that ran beneath the Thames. To Dirk, it was an entrance.

It was a long jump from the building and Dirk would never have risked it in daylight, but it was dark and he didn't want to waste any more time. He spread his wings, stood on his hind legs and jumped, gliding silently through the night sky, across the road, landing safely inside the vent. He found a door, opened it and stepped into the darkness. He felt along the wall and found a second door. He pushed it open and slid into a small stone room, not much bigger than a cupboard.

He said a few words in Dragonspeak and the small room plummeted into the depths of the earth.

When it finally stopped moving, Dirk saw in front of him a large ornate door carved into the shape of a dragon's head, with blood-red jewels set into its eyes and a ring through its nose. He jumped up, took the ring in his mouth, pulled it back and let it go. The bang echoed around the chamber and the door creaked open.

The hall behind was even more impressive than the door itself, lined with great stone pillars carved into the shapes of various creatures. There was a Vibria, a Wyvern, a Gogmagog, breeds of creatures that humans had branded mythological, each one sitting upright with its head tilted back and mouth wide open. Red flames burnt tirelessly from each mouth, illuminating the rock ceiling.

This was Karnataka's home, deep beneath the surface of London, far from the sunlight. The impressive hall was a stark contrast to Karnataka himself, a miserable no-good cowering coward with the morals of a Two-Toothed Fire Toad.

Dirk stopped by a giant stone snake with a large head and a long mane. It was an Amphiptere, like the one he and Holly had rescued from the Thames. He wondered again why Holly hadn't been in touch. In befriending a human, he had breached the forbidden divide, risking banishment if he was found out, but Dirk didn't care much for rules and regulations. Holly was his friend.

A thunderous voice boomed, 'Stop. Who enters this hall?'

First-time visitors might have been scared by the impressive sound, but Dirk knew it was nothing more than a cone-shaped voice projector, that transformed

Karnataka's thin nasal whine into the huge voice that filled the hall.

'I'm in no mood for the whole big-ego greeting, Karny,' yelled Dirk threateningly.

There was a brief pause and then the voice spoke again: 'Please leave! You are trespassing.'

The flames from the statues died down and two red eyes appeared in the darkness.

'You're not scaring me with your big pretend eyes, Karny,' taunted Dirk, peering into the darkness. 'Karny?' He walked towards the red lights.

'Turn around, Mountain Dragon,' said the voice threateningly. 'You are not welcome.'

Dirk sprang into action. He darted forward, past the two false eyes, and raised himself on to his hind legs, drawing his claws.

'You're not Karnataka,' he said.

Behind the wall was a Shade-Hugger, all right, with his brown back and caramel belly, but it wasn't Karnataka. He was thinner than Karny, with large fearful eyes. In a lilting voice he said, 'Please don't hurt me.'

'Where's Karnataka?' demanded Dirk. 'Who are you?'

'My name's Grendel Sheving. I'm Karny's cousin. I came down from the Midlands to visit but he's not here. Are yow with the Dragnet?'

'Do I look like a Drake?' said Dirk. The Dragnet was the dragon police force. Its officers were Drab-Nosed Drakes – wingless dragons with big bellies and short tails. 'Where has he gone?'

'He's legged it. The Dragnet have a warrant out for his arrest. I'm looking after the place while he's away,' said the dragon, gazing up at the rows of statues. 'It's a bit over the top, but it's a lot more spacious than my place under Dudley. I could get used to this.'

Dirk could think of a whole string of reasons why the Dragnet might be after Karnataka, but he had always figured that Karny was too smart, or too slippery, to get found out.

Grendel limped out from behind the voice projector and whispered, 'There are mutterings of a Kinghorn revolt. There's a new captain at Dragnet and he's arresting half the dragon world on suspicion of being Kinghorns.'

'How do you know all this?'

'Everyone knows,' replied Grendel. 'Where have yow been? They're filling up the cells with suspects. The Council have been called.'

The Dragon Council was made up of the six oldest living dragons, all of whom were very old and extremely forgetful. As Dragon Law required all six councillors for a trial to take place, accused dragons often waited years for their cases to come up, while the councillors came and went, forgetting where they were supposed to be or what they were supposed to be doing.

'What have they got on Karny?' asked Dirk.

'I don't know, but he's hardly got a clean slate, has he? He's a Cuddlums all right.'

'A what?' said Dirk.

'Oh, has he never told you his surname? He prefers all this Karnataka the Great, Karnataka the Brave.' Grendel laughed. 'Karnataka Cuddlums doesn't quite have the same ring, does it? Yes, trouble runs on that side of the family. Yow know what happened to Elsinor?'

'Karnataka told me, yes,' said Dirk.

Karnataka's brother, Elsinor, had been accused of attacking a remote human village in Romania several years ago. The incident had made the human press, but most right-minded humans had dismissed it as nonsense, knowing full well that dragons don't exist.

'What about you? Looks like you've been in the wars,' Dirk said, indicating Grendel's limp.

'Oh, this, it's nothing,' said Grendel, sitting down.

'I don't suppose you have been leaping around the

38

city recently, have you?' asked Dirk, reading the Shade-Hugger for any signs of guilt.

'Breaching the forbidden divide? No way, matey,' replied Grendel, a look of fear in his eyes. 'I don't want to join them Cuddlumses in the Inner Core.'

Elsinor had protested his innocence to the bitter end, but that hadn't stopped the Council finding him guilty and sending him on the last journey he would ever make, to the edge of the Outer Core, then swimming through the liquid fire and blinding light to the earth's Inner Core. No dragon had ever returned.

'What makes you think Karnataka's heading down to join his brother?'

'The Dragnet always catch their dragons eventually, don't they? I don't know what they've got on him but I'd bet my right claw that it's more than gold tax evasion. I was thinking of swapping the door knocker for a bell. What do yow think?'

'I think you shouldn't go changing things that don't belong to you, Shade-Hugger,' said Dirk.

He left Grendel considering interior decoration and walked thoughtfully back into the small stone room, wondering if Karnataka really could have been responsible for his bruised head. Of course he could. Karny would have bashed his own mother over the head with a plank of wood if there was a chance she might get in the way of one of his deals. At least Dirk had something on him now. *Cuddlums*, he thought, smiling to himself.

It was late by the time Dirk jumped through his office window. He landed softly in front of his desk. He shut the window, lowered the blinds, poured himself a large neat orange squash and flicked on the TV.

A smarmy presenter was grilling a dull-looking politician, wearing a fixed smile.

'How can you justify the amount spent on defence when you can't tell me what that money is being spent on?' asked the presenter, leaning forward eagerly.

The politician gave a false laugh and said, 'My dear Jonathan, issues of defence are necessarily secret. Surely even you must understand that.'

'What about this leaked document on the AOG project? Can you tell me about that?'

Dirk noticed a twinge of irritation cross the minister's face. 'There is no such thing as the AOG project. That document was a fake, probably put around by one of your journalist lot in order to damage our election campaign.'

'What does AOG stand for?'

'I have no idea. I have already told you, to the best of my knowledge there is no such project.'

'Well, we've run out of time. Thank you, minister,' said the presenter, moving on to the next topic.

Dirk switched off the TV and threw the remote at what he thought was a cushion, but turned out to be Willow, who screeched and ran under the desk.

The professor had mentioned the AOG project. Knocking back the contents of the glass of orange squash, Dirk wondered what the professor did all day at that computer on the sixth floor of his Moorgate office. With this thought, he cleared away the baked-bean cans and old newspapers and settled down to sleep on his mattress.

Chapter Five

Holly struggled to get free. 'Who are you?' she demanded.

'I'll tell you on the way back to the dorm, Holly.' The girl pulled off Holly's makeshift balaclava, keeping a firm grip of her shoulder.

'I'm not going back. I'm leaving.'

'Well, go ahead, then,' said the girl, letting go and handing her the wire cutters, 'But I should warn you that as soon as you cut this wire you'll have the whole of security down on you faster than a tobogganing tadpole.'

Holly faltered. 'But . . . why?'

'This is no ordinary fence. It's made from SM2,

intelligent metal. Stuff they use in proper defence bases. Cutting it, climbing it or tunnelling under it triggers the alarm. And say you do get past it, you're tagged. The wristbands all have short-range tracking devices. They were introduced last year after one of the oh-so-famous students was kidnapped. That's why you can't take them off.'

'I was going to cut it off with the wire cutters.'

'Try it. You can't cut through them, you can't bite through them. It's easier to chop off your own hand than remove these babies.'

'But I thought all this security was to stop people getting in?'

'There are two types of pupils at William Scrivener: those being protected from the outside world and those being kept from the outside world. Have a guess which you are. Let's get you back to bed. The security guards know not to hurt the students but the dogs haven't been as well trained. I heard one bit a student the other day.'

The girl led Holly back towards the dorm, walking in the shadows of the trees.

'It took me three attempts before I figured out the tree walk. I watched you practising during breaks. More difficult in the dark, isn't it? I used to practise blindfolded. I reckon I can get across those trees as quickly as anyone can walk along the path. My name's Moji, by the way.'

'Are you going to report me?' asked Holly.

'Not this time,' said Moji. 'You've only been here a month, haven't you?'

'Yes. I got sent here to stay out of trouble.'

Moji laughed. 'You're doing a great job. What was your plan once you got out?'

'I was going to find a phone box and call a friend.'

'Someone by the name of Dirk Dilly?' said Moji, pulling out a handful of envelopes from her pocket and handing them back to her.

'You've been stopping my letters,' said Holly angrily.

'Not me, the school. Palmer would never let anything that criticises the school get out in case the press got hold of it, not to mention what you say about poor Petal. Who is this Dirk you're writing to then, an uncle or something?'

Holly smiled to herself, remembering how she had pretended to be Dirk's niece in order to get past his landlady into his office. 'Something like that,' she said.

'The school intercepted the mail and Palmer asked me to keep an eye on you.'

'Why you?'

'Because I know all the tricks in the book. I've made more attempts to get out of here than anyone else. I still hold the record for the furthest any student has ever got, all the way to Little Hope . . .' Moji stopped dead and pushed Holly hard against the tree, clasping her hand over her mouth. Holly struggled to get free, but Moji whispered, 'Be quiet. The guard's coming.'

Holly heard the crackling sound of a crowd roaring and a voice saying, '. . . a triumphant return to form for the Arsenal . . .' The guard must have left the channel open, so he could listen to the match.

Once he had passed, Moji released her and they continued on their way.

'So why won't you let me go?' asked Holly. 'We could go together.'

'My escaping days are over. I'm a prefect now, a respectable student of William Scrivener School. Besides, this is my last year here.'

The two girls got to the courtyard and Moji strolled across with Holly by her side. Reaching the door to the girls' dorm, Moji raised her wristband but stopped and said, 'On second thoughts, let's use Palmer's.'

She held out her hand. Holly looked up into her smiling face, pulled out the wristband and handed it to her.

'Good steal by the way,' said Moji, opening the door,

'but you forgot that there's a camera in Palmer's office.' They entered the building. 'And in the technical design room,' she added, holding out her hand again.

Holly handed over the wire cutters.

The security cameras swivelled to follow them as they headed down the corridor. They stopped by the notice board outside the common room. 'This is where we say goodbye,' said Moji.

'How do you know I won't try again?' replied Holly.

'Go ahead and try. I like a challenge,' countered Moji. 'But while you're on this side of the fence, you've got very little hope of ever making it.'

Moji winked at her, turned on her heel and walked away.

Holly felt depressed. She felt trapped. She looked up at the notice board and read.

PREFECT NOTICE

NEXT THURSDAY ALL PREFECTS WILL BE REQUIRED TO ACT AS USHERS AT THE SCHOOL CONCERT TAKING PLACE AT LITTLE HOPE VILLAGE HALL. NO PUPILS OTHER THAN BAND MEMBERS MAY ATTEND. THIS WILL BE A MEDIA EVENT SO SMART DRESS AND BEST BEHAVIOUR ARE REQUIRED.

PRINCIPAL PALMER

Holly thought about what Moji had said. She had lit-tle hope of getting out while she was on this side of the fence.

That was the answer. Moji was giving her a clue as to how to escape. She had to go to the concert and begin her escape from Little Hope.

A plan was already formulating in Holly's mind. She smiled and looked up at the camera. She took two steps back and it followed her. She stepped forward and it moved again. She jumped to the right then to the left, then again. The camera looked like it was having a fit. Holly giggled and ran back to her room, where she slipped back to bed, careful not to wake Petal.

Chapter Six

Dirk was drowning in an ocean of baked beans. He struggled to swim, but the beans were pulling him down. Tomatoey sauce filled his nostrils. The more he fought the deeper he sank.

'Mr Dilly?' screamed the beans. 'Hello, Mr Dilly?'

He awoke from the nightmare to find himself in his office with an empty baked-bean tin on the end of his nose. Willow was jumping over cans and old case files like it was a game.

I seriously need to clean up, he thought.

He looked up at the clock and scratched his head. He knew it shouldn't be difficult, but dragons didn't have a way of measuring time and Dirk had never quite got to grips with the bizarre system that humans used. Maybe it was time to go digital.

'Mr Dilly? Are you in?' Mrs Klingerflim was pounding on the door.

'I'll have the money next week,' called Dirk.

'Oh, don't worry about the rent, dear. I was hoping you might be able to help me with some lifting downstairs.'

He opened the door to find the old lady, smiling benignly.

'No problem, Mrs K,' he said.

'That's very kind, dear,' she replied. 'My Ivor used to do all the lifting. That's another thing he hasn't been able to do since he passed away.'

Dirk followed the old lady downstairs, careful that his tail didn't knock any of the old black-and-white pictures and china ornaments that lined the walls. He often wondered what the world looked like to Mrs K. If she was short-sighted enough not to realise that her unreliable tenant was in fact a 1,266 year-old red-backed, green-bellied, urban-based Mountain Dragon, the world must have been a pretty weird-looking place to her.

She led him into the kitchen, where there were two cardboard boxes on the floor.

'If you could put them on that top shelf,' she said. 'I'd do it myself but I'm not as tall as I used to be. It's a funny to-do, growing old. When you're young you get taller, then when you're middle-aged you get fatter. And, just when you're getting used to how tall and fat you are, bish bash bosh, you're old, thin and short. It's a bit like being an inflatable castle.'

'And life's one big kid's birthday party,' mused Dirk, picking up one of the boxes. It was full of dusty old books. He turned the top one over. It had a red cover with a thick white line that zigzagged across the front. 'Anything good to read in here?' he asked, holding it up.

'Oh no, just Ivor's old rubbish,' she replied. 'I'd throw it away but I find the older I get, the more sentimental I am about these knick-knacks.'

Dirk put the book back in the box and placed it on the shelf. He stooped to pick up the second box and noticed on the dining table a gleaming computer. It looked strangely out of place in Mrs Klingerflim's kitchen.

'I see you're moving with the times,' he said.

'Silly, isn't it?' she replied. 'My eldest, Mark, bought it for me, said I needed updating. He connected up all the wires and things. Broad-bean connection, he said, but what's an old lady like me going to do with that? I get my broad beans from the corner shop.'

'Can I have a look?' asked Dirk, placing the second box on the shelf by the first.

'Of course, dear. I'll put the kettle on.'

He moved the chair out of the way and sat down in front of the computer, ever cautious not to let his scaly skin brush against the old lady.

Human technology wasn't really Dirk's strong point, but computers had their uses and the Internet could be great for getting information on suspects. He moved the mouse and found a search engine. Using the tip of his claw he carefully typed in the company name NAPOW.

An expensive-looking website appeared on screen. Dirk read the company description.

NAPOW is a world-class supplier of electronic warfare systems and cutting-edge defence technology.

So that's what the professor did, he made weapons, and fairly heavy-duty ones by the look of the website. A globe materialised in the centre of the screen and the company motto appeared.

NAPOW:
MAKING THE WORLD A SAFER PLACE

Dirk smiled to himself. It was typical of humans. A company dedicated to creating the very latest in destructive technology, capable of killing greater numbers at higher speed with less effort, and that made the world safer.

'Tea, dear?' asked Mrs Klingerflim.

'No, thanks,' said Dirk.

He tried another search, on 'AOG project', and found various newspaper articles referring to it as some sort of secret government defence project, but nothing that said what it was, or that connected it with NAPOW.

Mrs Klingerflim switched on the radio and some old crackly music came on.

'Oh, I like this one,' said the old lady, moving strangely to the music. 'It reminds me of my Ivor. He used to take me out dancing to tunes like this all night long. They don't write them like they used to.'

It sounded awful to Dirk but then he hated all music. For dragons, music was not something you listened to for fun. Dragonsong was a powerful and deadly weapon.

He heard the phone in his office start ringing, so he thanked Mrs Klingerflim for the use of the computer and went upstairs. He shut the door with his tail and answered the phone.

'Hi,' he said, scooping up Willow and stroking her.

'Mr Dilly? Is that you?' said an anxious female voice.

'What can I do for you, Mrs Rosenfield?' he asked.

'I was wondering if you'd found anything yet ...' Her voice wavered. 'It feels so underhand hiring you. I love my husband, Mr Dilly, but I'm scared.'

'Why? What's happened?' asked Dirk.

'He says that he's got one of his conferences this weekend, that he forgot to tell me about it, but he's lying.'

'Why do you think he's lying?'

'Someone called last night. I listened in on the other phone. The man told Karl to get the 8.59 train from Euston to Glasgow, but Karl told me he was going from King's Cross.'

'What did the voice sound like?' asked Dirk.

'Deep,' she replied. 'Like a soul singer.'

'What else did it say?'

'I only caught the end of the conversation. He said that Karl wasn't actually going to Glasgow, but that he would receive a phone call telling him when he should get off the train and that someone would be there to meet him. We've been married . . . for . . .' She began to cry. 'For . . . twenty-three years.'

Dirk hated the sound of humans crying.

'Mrs Rosenfield,' he said gently, 'people lie for lots of reasons. Don't jump to any conclusions. I'll find out what he's doing. Don't worry.'

'Thank you, Mr Dilly,' she sniffed.

'What sort of conference did he say it was?'

'He said it was one of his nonsense cryptozoological conferences.'

'Cryptozoological?'

'It's stupid, really, just his hobby, mythical creatures, he loves anything like that . . . unicorns, sea monsters and, you know . . .'

'Dragons?' said Dirk.

'Yes, they're his favourite. That's why I chose your detective agency. In a funny sort of way I thought he'd approve of the name . . .' Her voice trailed away.

'Why didn't you mention this before?' asked Dirk.

'I didn't think it was relevant. It's just a stupid hobby, isn't it? Those things don't really exist, do they?'

'Of course they don't. It just helps to know these things sometimes,' said Dirk. 'I'll call when I have news.'

He put down the receiver and looked up at the

clock. The big hand was pointing left. The smaller hand was below it. He scratched his head.

Come on, Dirk, you can do this, he thought. Big hand was minutes. Yes. That meant it was a quarter to something. The small hand was hours and that was just below the nine. That was it. A quarter to nine.

A quarter to nine? He had less than fifteen minutes to get to Euston Station. Dirk was quick but even he couldn't get across London's roofs at that speed, particularly not in daylight on a busy Saturday morning.

He pulled open the window, checked the street below and leapt out. It was a bright day, but overcast, like a grey blanket was spread over the sky. Usually Dirk travelled over roofs because they provided good cover. If he was seen he could stop and blend in an instant, disappearing from sight. He could become a figment of your imagination quicker than you could say, 'Oh, look, a dragon sitting on top of Tesco's.' However, Dirk had a good pair of wings and was perfectly capable of flying. He just had to take precautions in a big city like London.

He shut his mouth and snorted through his nostrils, standing upright on his hind legs and spinning round. White smoke billowed out of his nose. He flapped his wings as he turned, sending the smoke into a cloud that swirled around his body. He flapped a little harder, lifting himself off the roof, twisting and snorting as he flew upwards, to keep the smoke around him.

Having reached a good height, Dirk allowed the smoke to thin out to see where he was going. The view was spectacular, his beloved city of London at his feet. He found Euston and headed, feet first, towards it. Seeing an aeroplane flying above, Dirk snorted hard to thicken the smoke screen.

Inside the aeroplane, one of the passengers, also admiring the view of London, noticed the strange clump of smoke floating across the city.

'Take a look at this,' she said, tapping her boyfriend, who was pretending to be asleep. 'This cloud is acting very oddly.'

'Is it really? How very interesting, dear,' said the boyfriend, patting her hand, not bothering to open his eyes.

Wondering whether she should break up with her sarcastic boyfriend and instead go out with the nice chap she had met down the laundrette, the girlfriend forgot all about the peculiar cloud drifting across London.

Dirk landed on the corrugated roof above the station

platforms and the smoke wafted away.

Above the sound of the train engines starting up, whistles blowing and doors shutting, an announcement said, 'The train about to depart from platform seven is the 8.59 to Glasgow. Please stand clear of the platform's edge . . .'

The train rumbled forward.

There was no time to think.

Dirk sprang into the air, spread his wings and glided down, landing safely on top of the moving train, holding on tight and blending with the carriage roof.

Chapter Seven

Holly had been learning the trumpet for two years but had never stayed long enough at any one school to have proper lessons, so had taken to teaching herself from a book, on her own, in her room. She wasn't very good but it was noisy and she liked to play when she felt lonely because it filled the room with sound. But if she was going to persuade the music teacher, Miss Gilfeather, to let her join the band so late, she would have to play her very best.

Trumpet case in hand, she entered the small room labelled MUSIC ROOMS. It was Saturday morning when pupils had one-to-one music lessons, so Holly had decided to wait until Miss Gilfeather had a spare moment then ask if she could join the band. She could hear a flute and a piano playing a piece of classical music behind another door. Or rather, the piano was playing. The flute was desperately trying and failing to keep up.

She looked for somewhere to sit and saw that she wasn't alone. By the side of an upright piano was a skinny boy, sitting so still that she hadn't noticed him at first. Greasy black hair was flattened against his forehead. He didn't look at her but she saw his grip tighten round the handle of his curved instrument case, as though afraid she might steal it.

'Hi, I'm Holly,' she said, sitting down next to the boy. 'Is that a French horn?'

His dark eyes flickered nervously to look at her.

She tried again, offering her hand and saying, 'I play the trumpet. I want to join the band. Are you in the band?'

The strange boy made a noise somewhere between a giggle and a squeak and brought a hand up to his face, compulsively smoothing down his already very smooth hair.

Holly decided to give it one more try. 'I've never played in front of anyone before. I taught myself. What about you?'

When the boy answered he spoke quickly without pausing for breath. 'I have lessons, but the teachers get scared, everyone gets scared. They don't like being in a room with Callum, they think Callum is weird, but I still play because music blocks out the other noises. I never wanted to join the stupid band because other people aren't as good and spoil it and I hate it when people play wrong notes, like that flute in there, but Father thinks the concert will show people that Callum isn't a nutcase and so I have to be in the stupid band.'

The boy took a sharp intake of breath and smoothed down his hair.

Before Holly could respond, the door was flung open by a severe-looking woman, immaculately dressed in a trouser suit, holding a flute at arm's length, as though it was the most repulsive object she had ever touched.

She walked to the bin and dropped in the instrument.

Petal Moses darted out of the room and dived to the flute's rescue. 'How dare you?' she demanded. 'My mother bought that for me. It's an antique. It's worth more than you earn in a year.'

'That's probably true, Miss Moses,' the teacher admitted. 'And yet in your hands it may as well be a penny whistle. I told you last week that if you didn't practise that this would be your last lesson.'

'If you're so good at music, why aren't you a proper musician like my mum, rather than just a music teacher?' Petal snarled.

Miss Gilfeather emitted a very precise laugh in a 2/4 rhythm. 'My dear, your mother is a pop star, not a musician.'

'My mother has won awards,' Petal screamed, 'and I'm gong to call Mum and get a record contract and then you'll see.'

'I'm sure you will,' said Miss Gilfeather, maintaining her composure. 'The pop charts are full of talentless chimpanzees. Now, kindly leave. You have wasted enough of my time.'

Petal swung round and saw Holly. 'What are you staring at?' she demanded.

'I think you'd better give your psychiatrist a call too,' replied Holly.

'Hermann is a therapist,' replied Petal. 'It's Callum that needs a psychiatrist, a whole team of them, I heard.' Petal pointed at the dark-haired boy. 'Crazy Callum, the Prime Minister's son.'

'Children, please don't argue in my rehearsal rooms,' said Miss Gilfeather. 'The acoustics are far too good to waste on shouting. If you wish to tear each other limb from limb, we have a perfectly good playground.'

Petal stormed out of the room, slamming the door as she left.

Holly had known that the Prime Minister's son was in the year above her, but she had expected him to be one of the super-confident, horse-riding rich kids that she hated so much.

'What a very highly strung young lady. Reminds me of a violin I once had,' said Miss Gilfeather, turning to look at Holly. 'Who are you?' she demanded. 'You are not scheduled for a lesson.'

'I'm Holly Bigsby. I'm new and I want to join the band.'

'Impossible,' replied the teacher. 'The concert is in five days' time.'

'I'm a quick learner. I only started the school recently and I was hoping the band would help me make friends.'

'It's not about making friends. It's about making music.'

'Please, at least give me an audition.'

Miss Gilfeather gave Holly a sustained stare and then spoke. 'Very well. I will give you an audition after Mr Thackley's lesson. Wait here.'

The boy followed her into the room and the door

shut behind them. The piano started again and the French horn joined in, hitting every note perfectly and playing with feeling and precision. It sounded beautiful. Holly was stunned.

After half an hour the door opened and the boy walked out, his instrument case clasped in his sweaty hands.

'Excellent, Mr Thackley, as usual. See you on Monday for band rehearsals,' said Miss Gilfeather. 'Now, Miss Bigsby, let's see what you can do.'

Holly got up nervously and went into the room. As she passed Callum he whispered, 'Good luck.'

'Close the door,' said Miss Gilfeather. 'What did you say your name was?'

'Holly Bigsby, miss.'

'Ah, yes, the terrible tearaway. Mr Palmer has mentioned you. Well, I don't care for rebellion in my band. Music is unique in being both a science and an art. It should be studied with the brain and played with the heart. I see you play trumpet. I will accompany you on this piece.'

She handed Holly a sheet of music.

'I brought my own piece to play,' replied Holly.

'If you are hoping to play in the concert you will have to demonstrate the ability to sight-read. Given enough time you can teach a monkey to play Mozart, but they'll never be able to sight-read.'

'You can teach a monkey to play Mozart?'

'Please familiarise yourself with the key and we'll begin.'

The music looked difficult, with three flats by the stave, plus a few more thrown in during the piece. Holly took her trumpet from her case and held it up to her lips. She got the first few notes in her head, working out the fingering, then nodded to Miss Gilfeather, who sat down at the piano and began to play.

At the end of the piece, Miss Gilfeather said, 'Well, Holly Bigsby, your embouchure is appalling, you hold the trumpet at the wrong angle, your timing is off and you seem determined to turn every first quaver into a semi-quaver.'

Holly said nothing.

'However,' she continued, 'you do have some flare for the instrument and you have determination.' She picked up a folder and handed it to her. 'We only have two trumpets at the moment, so if you can learn all this you may play third.'

'Brilliant,' said Holly, smiling.

'But be warned, I expect utter dedication from my musicians. If I think you are damaging the integrity of the music you will be out of this band before your lips can touch that mouthpiece, young lady. Hold it up straight and stick your chin out. Band rehearsal is on Monday after school and the concert takes place on Thursday, when we will spend the entire day at the concert hall.'

Holly thanked Miss Gilfeather and left. In the corridor she found Callum, apparently waiting for her, but when she got near he shrank away.

'I got in,' she said. 'I heard you play, you were amazing.'

'I like music, I like playing, it makes me feel safe,' he said. 'I heard you too. You made some mistakes.'

'Don't worry about that spoilt pop-star's daughter. She's just mean. She killed my pet mouse.'

'I don't care about her,' he replied. 'She doesn't know anything, but I know. I see too much. They all think Callum is mad because of the monsters in my head. They are all in my head, but they're real too.'

'Who?' asked Holly, concerned. 'What are you talking about?'

'The doctors don't say mad. They call it post traumatic stress instead. It's when you go mad because you've been through something horrible.'

'What happened to you?'

'They're in the trees. They look like trees. You think they are trees, then they move and they talk and they have wings and teeth and I know they're in my head, they're all imaginary. They took me before and they'll take me again. They'll come soon. They told me they would, but what does it matter if it's all in Callum's head? Callum can control it. That's what the doctors said. There's no such thing as monsters.'

'Callum, what are you saying?' asked Holly anxiously.

'No one believes Callum. No one does.'

'I want to help you,' she persisted.

'No one helps me.'

Holly reached for his arm, but he shrugged her off, turned round and hurried down the corridor.

'Callum, wait,' she called after him, but he quickened his pace, smoothing down his greasy black hair.

Chapter Eight

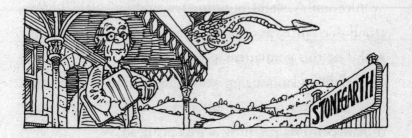

Looking at the green English countryside whizzing past the train, Dirk felt a tingle of nerves in his stomach. London was his home. It was where he felt safe. All this space made him feel uneasy.

The train had been travelling for a few hours when, finally, it stopped at a small village station with a sign that read Stonegarth, where Professor Rosenfield alighted, carrying the silver case. He looked up and down the empty platform. The train pulled away and Dirk jumped over Rosenfield's head on to the station roof. It was a bright, sunny day and Dirk was glad that dragons cast shadows upwards.

He peered over the other side of the roof. In the car

park of the station was an old yellow car, its paintwork chipped and eaten away by rust. Two men were leaning against the side of it. Dirk recognised them instantly.

'What's he a professor of, then?' said a short fat man with tightly curled red hair.

'Although a valid question, my tubby sidekick, I'm afraid that Mr G has not furnished me with a full biography of the gentleman concerned, so I will have to decline from honouring your inquisition with a satisfactory answer,' said the taller man with a merest wisp of hair combed carefully across his head.

'You mean, you don't know?'

'I am saying words to that effect, yes, Reg.'

It was the two idiot crooks who worked for the Kinghorns, Arthur and Reg. They had no idea that the Mr G they spoke of was in fact a dragon, the mysterious Vainclaw Grandin.

'Mr G don't tell us much, do he?' said Reg. 'I still don't know what we were doing with all those cats.'

'He certainly likes to play his cards close to his chest, Reginald,' agreed Arthur, 'but remember, it was he who paid for the lawyer who got us off. We owe him a great deal.'

'We only got arrested because of him in the first place,' protested the fat man.

'Ah, look yonder, this must be the chap,' said Arthur, noticing Professor Rosenfield standing outside the station scratching his head.

Arthur walked towards him and extended a hand. 'Professor Rosenfield, I presume,' he said, grinning.

'Er, yes,' replied the professor, shaking Arthur's hand uncertainly.

'My name is Arthur and this big-boned gentleman is my colleague, Reg. We are here to provide vehicular transportation to your destination.'

Professor Rosenfield looked vaguely at the two men.

'We're the wheels,' added Reg. 'Don't worry. I don't understand half of what he's on about neither. The trick is not to get too bogged down in listening to the words.'

'I'm sure the professor understands me perfectly adequately,' said Arthur. 'He too is a man of learning.' He turned to Rosenfield, opened the back door of the car and said, 'Worry not, Reg has very little in the way of grey matter but he is fully familiarised in the ways of motorised wheel control.'

The professor looked at the crooks as though they had just landed from a different planet. 'Er . . . Are you sure it's me you're here to pick up?'

'I suppose there is a possibility that we have been sent to collect a different man with the same name as you from this exact spot, yes, but you would have to admit that it would be a staggering coincidence,' replied Arthur.

'Well, yes, I suppose so,' admitted the professor.

'In you go, then.' Arthur helped the professor into the back. 'Look at that, we're already discussing probability,' he said. 'It is nice to have civilised company for a change.'

'I know about probability,' said Reg. 'It's gamblin', ain't it?'

'You see what I have to put up with,' sighed Arthur.

The two men took their seats in the front and drove away.

Dirk followed, firstly using the roofs of the houses, then, when they reached the edge of town, flying low behind the hedgerows, keeping his wings out of sight from the road, but also watching out for any farmers who might see him. He skirted the edge of a field of cows that mooed fearfully at him and retreated to the other side of the field.

The road ran alongside a large lake and Dirk skimmed across the surface, dipping his claws in and causing water to spray up. He had forgotten how much fun proper flying could be. Maybe it was good to get out of London, after all.

The car took a road that cut through a dense forest over a small hill. Dirk flew over the trees, keeping the car in sight. At the base of the hill it turned on to a smaller dirt track that led deeper into the forest. At the end of the track was a rundown old cottage with black-and-white walls. The car stopped outside and all three men got out.

Dirk swooped down and ducked behind the low stone wall that surrounded the cottage.

'Well, Professor Rosenfield,' said Arthur, opening the professor's door. 'It has been a pleasure. As you can imagine, working mostly with Reg I am generally starved of intellectual discourse. Except on the subject of light ales from around the world, Reg has very little in the way of knowledge.'

The professor climbed out of the car, holding the silver case with both arms.

'Who did you say you worked for?' he asked.

'Sadly, we are not at liberty to divulge that particular piece of information, are we, Reg?'

'What? About working for Mr G? No, can't say a word,' replied Reg.

Arthur raised a hand and casually whacked Reg on the back of his head.

'Ow, what d'you do that for?'

'I must apologise for my colleague,' Arthur said to the professor. 'He is as foolish as he is fat.'

'But who is Mr G?' asked the professor. 'Is that the man with the deep voice?'

'Goodbye, professor,' said Arthur.

'Nice to meet you,' added Reg.

The two men got back in the car.

'Aren't you staying with me?'

'I'm afraid not,' replied Arthur. The engine started. 'Our instructions were to leave you here. We will return each morn to provide transportation for procurement of provisions. Come on, Reg, *allez!*'

'A what?'

'It means go, you nincompoop.'

Reg let the handbrake off and they drove away, leaving the professor to enter the cottage through its only door.

Dirk scurried forward. There were two windows on either side of the cottage. Looking through the nearest one, he could see that the cottage was small and squalid and what an estate agent might describe as 'full of potential'. In other words, it was falling apart. Rosenfield sat down on a rickety wooden chair and placed the silver case on the kitchen table. He pressed a button on the side of the case and the lid opened, blocking out the professor's face. Dirk needed to see what he was doing, but suddenly he felt a sharp pain shoot through his tail.

He looked round to see the silver bark-coloured skin of a Tree Dragon. Its teeth were clamped over Dirk's tail. Its pale green eyes were staring at him wildly.

Chapter Nine

Dirk tried to swing his tail, but the Tree Dragon's grip was firm, secured by its claws digging into the ground like roots. Its mossy teeth had penetrated the soft underside of his tail, drawing dark green blood. The pain was immense.

Dirk opened his mouth and sent a line of fire, singeing his own tail but forcing the Tree Dragon to release him. He leapt on to the dragon's back, pressing the tips of his claws against its throat.

'Who are you?' he whispered, not wanting to attract the professor's attention. 'Why did you attack me?'

'Get off me. You're ouching me.'

It was a female.

'Tell me and I'll get off your back,' replied Dirk, holding down the Tree Dragon's writhing limbs and digging his claws further in.

She screamed in agony.

'Who's there?' shouted the professor from inside the cottage.

Dirk released the Tree Dragon, who darted up an oak tree, her body twisting easily around the thick trunk, disappearing into the dense forest.

'Who's there? Show yourself,' yelled the professor, coming to the window.

Not wanting to be seen by a human, Dirk took after the Tree Dragon.

Tree Dragons are fast movers in their own territory where they can swing from tree to tree, so it was difficult to keep up. He followed her deep into the forest until she stopped, landing on a malformed dead tree in the centre of a clearing, illuminated by white sunlight cutting through the green leaves.

'What do you want to know, Mountain?' she said.

'Who are you?' panted Dirk, catching his breath.

'My name's Betula Pendula,' she replied.

'Charmed, I'm sure,' he said. 'Why did you attack me?'

'You were schnooking on the manuman.'

'You mean Professor Rosenfield?'

'What do you know about the manuman?' snapped Betula.

'Who are you working for, Bark-back?' snarled Dirk.

'That's enough interroquests,' she replied.

'If I don't get some answers I'm going to open my mouth and burn down that tree and you with it,' threatened Dirk.

Betula laughed and said, 'Come on, bark sisters.'

The tree began to move, branches slowly peeling away, dismantling itself, lowering Betula down to the ground and splitting into four more parts. What Dirk had taken for a tree was actually four more Tree Dragons balanced on top of each other like acrobats, each one with a different bark-coloured skin.

'These are my cofrienions,' said Betula, introducing the Tree Dragons as they arranged themselves into attack formation in front of Dirk. 'This is Buxus Sempervirens, Tilia Cordata, Salix Alba and Acer Campestre.'

'Pleased to meet you, ladies,' said Dirk, 'now, tell me what you're doing here.'

'Come on, let's schmunch him,' said Buxus, snapping her teeth viciously.

'Let me do it,' said Acer, who had a whitish back covered in fine ridges.

'No, Acer,' replied Betula angrily. 'We're all going to kill him. It's not about notches on your bark.'

'You've already had your go, Betula,' Acer replied. 'It's my turn.'

'You heard what Betula said,' added Salix, whose back was greeny red.

'Strush up, Salix,' snapped Acer. 'You're always siding with Betula.'

'Oh, just let her,' said Tilia, who was thinner and darker than the others. 'What harm will it do?'

'Yeah, let's go one on one, you and me, Bark-back,' challenged Dirk.

Five sets of pale green eyes glared at him.

'Oh, let's just get him,' said Betula, diving forward and whacking Dirk in the face.

He swiped at her with his tail, but she evaded him by somersaulting over his head. A second one came at him from the side. Dirk deflected the attack with a wing, but a third had already locked her jaws around his leg. Pain raced through his body. He lashed out his tail and whacked the dragon over the head. She released her grip, but more came at him, their sharp teeth latching on to his leg and tail.

There were too many of them and they were too quick.

Fire burst from Dirk's mouth, but one of the dragons landed heavily on his back. He fell to the ground and the fire went out in a puff of smoke. He felt his wings clamped down and blood pour from his cuts. Another landed on his shoulders, and stood on his jaw, preventing him from breathing fire.

Betula's face appeared in front of his. 'This is what you get for schnooking, Mountain Dragon,' she said, opening her mouth, to finish him off.

'Mmmaknghurn.' Dirk struggled to speak.

'What's that?' said Betula.

'Kill him,' said Acer, standing on his jaw.

'Mmmaknghurn,' Dirk tried again.

'What's he saying?' asked Betula.

Acer lifted her foot up so that Dirk could speak.

'I'm a Kinghorn. Vainclaw sent me,' he said.

'You're not confrienious with the boss,' said Betula scornfully, but Dirk could tell he had guessed right. They were working for Vainclaw.

'He sent me to check up on you. He doesn't want to leave such an important job to a bunch of no-good Tree Dragons.'

'I should kill you for saying that,' she hissed.

'Kill me, then,' said Dirk. 'I'm sure he won't hold it against you, killing a member of his family.'

'He's fablifising,' said Acer.

Salix, who had been biting his leg, let go and said, 'Vainclaw is a Mountain Dragon. It's possible.' Dirk could feel blood ooze from where she had been biting through.

'My name is Jegsy Grandin,' he said. 'I'm Vainclaw's nephew.'

'Prove it,' said Betula. 'Tell us what's so important about the manuman?'

'Don't try and trick me,' replied Dirk. 'Vainclaw only lets you know as much as you need to know. He doesn't trust you. You just do what you're told. Well, do that now and let me go.'

Betula snarled angrily and yelled, 'Release him.'

'No, let's kill him,' said Acer.

'We can't risk it. What if he's truthing?'

'Then we tell the boss that it was a happendent.'

'Oh yes, I'm sure he'll comprestand, us happendently schmunching a member of his family. Let him go.'

All four dragons released Dirk and he stood up, checking his injuries. Dark green blood oozed from his tail and legs. Every inch of his body screamed out in agony. He had to get away but the dragons had surrounded him. He straightened out his wings, and gave them a couple of tentative flaps. They hurt like hell but they seemed to be working OK.

'Don't try anything,' said Betula nervously.

'What's going on, Jegsy?' asked Salix. 'Why are we watching the manuman? When is the boss coming to see us himself?'

Dirk stretched out his tail and found a rotten branch, hollowed out by ants.

'I asked you a question,' she snapped.

'And I think I've got the answer,' he said.

In one deft movement, he flipped up the branch with his tail, caught it in his paw, and set the end alight with a flame from his mouth. He spun round with it, creating a ring of fire around him. Instinctively, the Tree Dragons jumped out of the way and Dirk shot into the air, dropping the burning branch and disappearing over the tree tops.

Although Tree Dragons were quick on the ground, their wings were smaller, making them slower in the air. Not that Dirk was exactly match-fit himself, with his damaged wings and legs. He could feel them nipping at his heels. He tucked his tail in to stop them from grabbing it and flew as fast as he could.

'I told you he was fablifising,' he could hear Acer shouting.

'Don't let him escapaway,' yelled Betula.

One of the dragons snapped at his wings. He thrashed his tail out and sent her flying down into the forest. He was nearing the road, where a large lorry was hurtling along. He swooped down.

'Somebody stop him,' screamed Buxus, 'he's heading for the big schweeler.'

But it was too late. Dirk sailed over the edge of the forest and landed safely on the lorry. He clung tightly to the top and glanced back. The Tree Dragons had stopped above the forest, not wanting to risk exposure in the human world. Dirk was exhausted. He blended with the lorry but he was tired. He needed somewhere to hide out and recover.

The lorry stopped at a two-way junction where a sign pointed left to Stonegarth and right to a place called Little Hope. Dirk smiled at the name. It seemed somehow appropriate. Then he noticed what was written below it.

William Scrivener School – 1 Mile
No Press Allowed

Chapter Ten

By Monday morning Holly was beginning to feel nervous about band rehearsal. She had practised all the pieces of music, but she was worried that she wouldn't be good enough and Miss Gilfeather would throw her out, ruining her chances of escape.

Her mood wasn't improved by the realisation that today was the first English class in which they would be studying Petal's book.

Miss Whittaker, the English teacher, wore a wide grin.

'Normally I'd ask who would like to read first,' she began, 'but I think, since we have the opportunity, we should hear it in the author's own voice. Petal?'

Petal stood up, matching Miss Whittaker's grin, and opened her book, carefully and proudly.

Holly stared out of the window at the large grounds, imagining herself running across the field and leaping over the high wire fence, trying to shut out the sound of Petal's voice.

"'Chapter one. My Wonderful Birth,'" Petal read. "'There had been much speculation over my mother's pregnancy. Was it a boy or a girl? What would she call it? What birth method would she choose?'"

'Who was the father?' muttered Holly under her breath, making the boy next to her laugh.

Miss Whittaker threw a stern glance at her.

Holly didn't care. And she didn't care about the media buzz that surrounded Petal's birth. She was thinking about Callum. Yesterday she had visited the library and used the computer to locate a series of newspaper articles about him. The first was from last year, when Callum would have been in year seven. It read:

PRIME MINISTER'S SON KIDNAPPED FROM SCHOOL

Yesterday, Scotland Yard confirmed that the Prime Minister's youngest son, Callum Thackley (11), has been kidnapped from his school grounds. Detective

83

Chief Inspector Arnold Stickler said, 'Callum Thackley was abducted three days ago during a lunch hour.'

Prime Minister James Thackley is yet to issue an official statement but is said to be 'deeply concerned'.

The self-styled Principal of the school, Larry Palmer, said he would do everything he could do to assist the police and that they would be investing in state-of-the-art security measures in order to avoid any repeat of such an event. 'I believe our parents should be able to treat William Scrivener's like a bank, placing their most valuable assets somewhere they will be safe,' said Palmer in a press conference.

So far, no terrorist organisation has come forward to claim the kidnap.

There were a number of articles along these lines until one appeared a few days later saying:

CALLUM THACKLEY FOUND UNHARMED

After days of national concern, Callum Thackley, the Prime Minister's son, has been found, metres away from the spot he was taken. Although deeply distressed, he is physically unharmed. Detective Chief Inspector Stickler, who has been leading the investigation, said: 'One of our officers discovered the boy sitting under a tree not far from the sight of the original abduction in the forest surrounding the school. After thoroughly combing the area, no suspects were found. Callum is understandably traumatised but is doing very well, considering.'

The Prime Minister issued

More articles followed, some suggesting that Callum never fully recovered from his kidnapping ordeal, others speculating as to the motive for the kidnapping and why no demands were made, but none of them indicated that the police ever did discover who was behind his abduction.

Callum didn't seem to have any friends at school. He was known as Crazy, Crackpot or Cuckoo Callum. Holly felt sorry for him. She knew what it was like to go through life without friends.

"'In the end it was a simple candlelit water birth,'" Petal continued in a sing-song voice, "'with positive energy provided by a choir of Buddhist monks, a bottle-nosed dolphin in the pool, and a thousand rose petals floating on the surface. On May the first, at eleven in the morning, Petal Dolphin Moses entered the world. I was healthy and I was beautiful. Unfortunately, the dolphin became so distressed by the sight of me being born that it began to attack my mother. Luckily one of the monks intervened, jumping into the pool and wrestling the dolphin until a vet arrived and had the poor creature put to sleep.'"

Petal sat down and Miss Whittaker led the class in a round of applause. 'Now,' she said, still giddy with excitement. 'Would anybody care to say what strikes them about that opening passage?'

Holly looked longingly out of the window at the bright sunny morning and for a moment she thought she saw something. No, she couldn't have. She blinked. It must have been her eyes playing tricks on her. She could have sworn . . . but how could she? It looked like Dirk. *No*, she said to herself, *you're just missing him*.

Her thoughts were interrupted by a nudge from the boy next to her and she saw that everyone was staring expectantly at her.

'Well?' said Miss Whittaker.

'I'm sorry, could you repeat the question?' asked Holly.

'I asked what you thought of the way the author uses humour in the opening passage,' she said.

'I think he wrote it very humorously,' said Holly simply.

The class laughed. Petal stared angrily at Holly as if willing her to drop dead.

'The author is a girl,' said Miss Whittaker patiently.

'Oh, I'm sorry,' said Holly, 'I thought you meant Bob,

the man she had write it for her.'

Before Miss Whittaker could say a word, Holly picked up her bag and headed off for her daily visit to the principal's office.

The principal's secretary, who today had her hair tied back and wore green nail varnish, told Holly that Principal Palmer was away all morning at a shareholders' meeting, so she returned to the class for the next lesson, which was games.

The class gathered on the field and Mr Brooker, a scruffy-looking man with a large, matted beard, announced that they would be practising cross-country running around the perimeters of the school grounds.

The class groaned. The blue sky had clouded over and a light drizzle hung in the air. It was a miserable day for a long run.

'Don't be soft. It'll put hairs on your chest,' said Mr Brooker. 'It'll put toad in your hole.' He jogged on the spot, then added, 'It'll put pay-as-you-go minutes in your mobile. Come on.'

'Excuse me, sir.' Petal Moses, dressed immaculately in her white designer gym kit, raised her hand.

'Yes, Petal,' said Mr Brooker.

'Fabio says he doesn't want me going on any long runs because of my weak ankle.'

'Is Fabio a doctor and did he write you a note?'

'No, sir, he's my personal trainer, but he's worked with some of the biggest names in Hollywood.'

'I'm sorry, Petal,' said Mr Brooker, the corners of his mouth curling into a smile. 'No note, no excuse. Let's go, my people.'

He ran round and herded the reluctant class like a sheepdog, guiding them along the side of the football pitch to the perimeter fence, where he explained that the run would take about forty-five minutes to an hour. 'If you run too slowly,' he added, 'you'll be late for lunch. There's your motivation.'

He blew a whistle and they set off, some of the class running full pelt, others jogging at a more sensible pace. Inevitably the class soon became spread out, naturally splitting into pairs or threes.

Not having any friends, Holly ran alone.

She saw Petal running ahead of her with two girls. She was pleased that Petal had been forced to do the run. It was miserable. The sky was dark and the rain-drops were getting larger every minute, soaking their clothes. The ground softened and soon Holly could feel mud beneath her trainers.

She decided to overtake Petal, speeding up to run between her and the fence. As she approached she could hear her saying, 'Fabio says running without a running machine is like wearing boot-cut jeans to a launch party. No one does it any more . . . A-choo.' She sneezed. 'That's it. I'm catching a cold. As soon as I get back I'm calling my lawyer. I'm going to sue the school.'

Holly drew level with Petal, who looked round and said, 'Oh, hi, Holly. How's your boyfriend, Crackers Callum?'

'He's not my boyfriend,' replied Holly.

She sped up, but Petal kept level, saying, 'Holly loves crazy Callum, the Prime Minister's son.'

The other girls giggled.

'I do not,' yelled Holly.

She ran faster, but Petal and her friends kept up.

'Stands to reason,' said Petal. 'They're both freaks.'

'At least I'm not a . . .' started Holly, but her retort was cut short as she felt something collide with her shin. She stumbled and fell, losing her balance and landing face down in the mud.

The three girls laughed and Petal shouted, 'Enjoy your trip?'

A pair of boys ran past her without stopping to check that she was all right. Holly felt miserable. She was wet. She was cold. She was muddy. She felt lonely and humiliated. Then she heard a voice say, 'Stay where you are. Let the stragglers pass.'

On the other side of the fence two large yellow eyes were staring at her.

'Dirk?' she gasped. 'Is it really you?'

Chapter Eleven

Holly let the last few runners pass. None stopped to ask if she was all right or if she needed a hand up.

Once they were gone, she said, 'What are you doing here?'

'I was in the neighbourhood,' said Dirk, before adding, 'I can see you're as popular as ever.'

'I'm so glad to see you,' said Holly. 'Not that I can see you really.'

She could just about make out Dirk's outline, although his skin was perfectly blended with his surroundings. He shifted and the colour returned to his body.

'How's that?' he asked.

'Be careful. They have cameras everywhere.'

'It's a blind spot,' replied Dirk.

Holly checked. It was true. A large tree overhanging the fence blocked the nearest camera, and a high hedgerow stood between them and the school building. Holly saw that he had slipped his tail through a hole in the fence to trip her up. Patches of dark green liquid oozed from Dirk's tail and legs. Some of it had rubbed off on her shin when he tripped her. She touched it. It was sticky and thick. Instinctively, she put it to her tongue and, in spite of its colour, recognised the metallic taste as blood.

'You're bleeding,' she said. 'What happened?'

'I ran into another one of Vainclaw's little armies.' Dirk sounded tired, his breathing was heavy and the smoke from his nostril had an unhealthy yellow hue. 'Tree Dragons. Vicious creatures.'

Holly heard a dog barking nearby.

'Did you make that hole?' she asked.

'Yep, bit straight through.'

'We haven't got much time. The guards are coming. They can tell when the fence has been cut.'

'I should get out of here,' said Dirk.

'What are you going to do?' said Holly, worried. She hadn't seen Dirk look so bad since he was knocked

unconscious after swallowing poisonous Amphiptere
blood.

'Don't worry about me. I've looked worse than this.
Dragon skin is tough stuff. It'll heal as I sleep. There are
some caves on the other side of the forest where I can
lie low long enough to heal up. A good night's rest and
I'll be fine. Why don't you come with me, help me
solve this case?'

Holly wanted nothing more than to go with him, but
she touched her wristband, sighed and said, 'I can't. They'll
track me down. Come to Little Hope on Thursday.
There's a big concert and I'm going to escape then.'

The barking dog was getting nearer.

Holly said, 'I did write to you, but they stopped the
letters.'

Dirk smiled. 'I thought you'd forgotten about me.'

'Forgotten about you?' said Holly. 'You're a red-
backed, green-bellied, urban-based Mountain Dragon,
who works as a detective. How could I forget you?
Besides, we're friends, aren't we?'

'Sure we are,' replied Dirk.

They could hear the static crackle from the guard's
radio.

'Hide,' urged Holly and Dirk's skin blended with the
ground.

'Hey, lassie, what are you doing?' shouted a voice.

Holly looked up to see a thickset man with a black bushy moustache in a security uniform.

'I fell over while running and sprained my ankle,' she said.

In one hand, the guard had a walkie-talkie. In the other, he held back a rather angry-looking poodle, which barked at the invisible dragon he could smell on the other side of the fence.

'Did you make this hole?' asked the guard.

'Aren't guard dogs usually German Shepherds or Rottweilers?' said Holly, looking at the poodle.

'Oh, aye, but one of the dogs attacked a student last week, nothing serious, just a wee bit of mauling. But the school board has insisted we use less-aggressive dogs. He's called Bruno.'

'Hello, Bruno,' said Holly to the perplexed poodle.

'Does it noh look stupid, me with a poodle?'

'Not at all,' lied Holly. 'He seems quite . . . well, barky.'

'Aye, Ah've bin trying to increase his aggression levels, using North American war chants and a sophisticated Pavlovian behavioural technique involving energy bars, Irn-Bru and spam.'

'Looks like it's working,' said Holly.

'Noh really. Shut up, Bruno. Now, did you make this

hole?' asked the guard pointing to the fence.

'No, it was here when I fell,' said Holly truthfully.

'I see. It's probably another wee creature gnawing through it again.'

Holly smiled, thinking if only he knew what sort of 'wee' creature it was that had made the hole.

'Right, come on, then, let's get you back to school.'

She followed the guard back and noticed that his name badge read 'Hamish Fraser'.

'So, Hamish,' she said, 'how do you know when there's a hole in the fence?'

'An alarm goes off in the security cabin,' he replied.

'What else can you control from the cabin?' she asked innocently.

'Almost everything,' said the guard.

'But the cameras are activated by movement, aren't they?'

'Oh, aye, but you can override everything from inside. It's like the bridge of the starship blinking enterprise in there,' he said. 'Noh like in my day. All this electronic nonsense. You can't beat a man with a good pair of eyes and proper guard dog. Sorry, Bruno.'

After an afternoon of boring classes, during which Petal took every opportunity to make some snide remark about Holly being in love with crazy Callum, it was band rehearsal, so Holly picked up her trumpet and headed for the rehearsal room.

Standing outside, listening to all the instruments warming up, she felt the unmistakable flutter of nerves. Focusing on the plan she took a deep breath and entered.

The large rehearsal room was full of students and instruments and noise. In one corner a group of older girls in flowing skirts practised trills on their flutes. In another, three large boys were making fart noises with trombones and laughing very loudly. She spotted two boys holding trumpets, and introduced herself.

'Hi, I'm Holly,' she said, opening her case. 'I'm third trumpet.'

'Hello,' said one of the boys, offering his hand formally. 'I'm Julian. This is Sandy.'

Holly shook his hand.

'I am second trumpet because I can reach top C and Jules is first trumpet because he can reach F above top C. What's your highest note?'

'Er . . .'

Holly was grateful that Miss Gilfeather entered the room, holding a baton and saying, 'Everyone take your places, please.'

The band assembled. Holly looked at the French horns and saw Callum smoothing down his hair, avoiding eye contact with anyone.

With everyone settled, Miss Gilfeather addressed the band.

'Welcome everyone. As you know, this Thursday is our school concert and tradition dictates that this takes place at Little Hope, even though we have perfectly adequate facilities here. This will attract the usual media hullabaloo and Mr Palmer has asked me to remind you to look smart. Personally I don't care if you dress up in monkey costumes as long as you play the notes correctly. Now, let's begin with the music you have on your stands.'

Everyone lifted their instruments, but before they could start, the doors swung open and three men in dark suits and dark sunglasses moved quickly and purposefully into the room.

'What is it?' snapped Miss Gilfeather.

One of the men whispered something in her ear, while the other two surveyed the room.

'Can't it wait until after rehearsal?'

Again the man said something inaudible. Miss Gilfeather replied, 'This is very inconvenient,' before announcing, 'Callum Thackley. Please come forward.'

Holly looked over to Callum, who had shrunk down in his seat, smoothing his hair and looking at the floor.

The men marched across the room towards him. One snatched the French horn from his hands, while the others grabbed Callum, holding him between them, dragging him towards the door.

'No,' screamed Callum, kicking and screaming. 'Don't let them take me. I don't want to go.'

Miss Gilfeather said, 'Oh, for goodness' sake, Callum. They work for your father. They are taking you to a photo call at Number 10.'

'I don't want to go. They can't take Callum. I don't want to miss the concert.' He kicked and struggled, but the man lifted him and carried him across the room.

'They've assured me you'll be back for the concert.'

Callum wasn't listening. He was screeching, 'The tree creatures. They're coming for me. Don't let them take me. They want me.'

Tree creatures, thought Holly and something clicked into place. Dirk said that there were Tree Dragons in the forest. What if Callum wasn't making it up? What if the tree creatures that kidnapped him weren't inventions of his troubled imagination but real dragons? What if these men weren't from the government at all, but working for the Kinghorns? What if they were kidnapping Callum again?

'Leave him alone,' she shouted, making Julian and Sandy jump.

'Holly Bigsby, sit down,' ordered Miss Gilfeather.

The three men had got Callum out of the room, and Holly could hear his pleas for help down the corridor.

'If you ask me he's one note short of a full scale, that one,' said Julian, causing Sandy to giggle.

'Now, if we could please start rehearsal,' said Miss Gilfeather, raising her baton.

Holly lifted her trumpet to her lips, but when the band started she missed her first note, so mimed along with Julian and Sandy. Her mind wasn't on the music. It was on Callum. She had to help him. If Callum had got mixed up with the world of dragons and everyone thought he was mad then Holly was the only one who knew the truth. Dragons did exist.

She had to get out and find Dirk and she could no longer wait until the concert on Thursday. But if she was going to make a clean break, she would have to find a way of removing the non-removable wristband.

Chapter Twelve

Walking back to the girl's dorm, Holly formulated a plan. She needed to make a phone call on a clean line and remembered Petal boasting that her mobile phone wasn't monitored because her mother didn't want anyone listening to their conversations.

She put her trumpet back in her room and headed for the common room, where she found Petal regaling a cluster of older girls with the story of when her mother had come home drunk with a Hollywood A-list star. Holly had heard the story a number of times but she listened patiently until the end, laughing along with the others, before saying, 'Petal, can I talk to you?'

Petal's smile fell away. 'What do you want now?'

'I wanted to say sorry,' said Holly. 'It's just that I think I am a bit jealous like your therapist, Hermann, said. And I really like your mum's new album and I think your book is brilliant. Can we be friends?'

Petal eyed her suspiciously for a moment then her smile returned and she opened her arms. Holly leaned in and they hugged. Petal whispered in her ear, 'I forgive you.'

'Thanks, Petal. It means the world to me,' said Holly. With convincing tears in her eyes she excused herself from the room.

As she walked away she could hear Petal saying, 'That's a turn-up for the books but I knew no one could really dislike me. I knew she was jealous.'

Outside the room, Holly smiled and pulled Petal's mobile phone out of her pocket.

She dialled a number she had memorised and listened to it ring, anxiously watching the door. Petal wouldn't take long to realise that her precious mobile phone was missing. The call went through to an answering machine and Holly left a message, finishing just as the common room door burst open and Petal appeared.

'You stole my phone, you cow!' she yelled.

'Here you go,' said Holly, handing it back to her.

Petal spent the rest of the evening threatening to report Holly as a thief, so when an announcement came over the loud speaker the next day, asking her to come to the principal's office, Holly assumed that she must have done so.

The principal's secretary looked bored, as she carefully painted her nails black and white to match the chequered dress she was wearing.

She held up a black-nailed finger, indicating that Holly should wait, and pressed a white-nailed finger on the intercom button. 'Holly Bigsby is here, principal,' she said in her usual flat tone.

Holly heard the principal's voice mid-laugh, say, 'Send her in, Angie.'

'He's in a good mood, stock must be up,' said the secretary, unsmiling.

Holly entered the office to find the principal sitting behind his desk wearing a smart pinstriped suit, and a matching shirt and tie, in mid-conversation with a man, sitting opposite him.

'Diversify or die, as they say,' said the man, laughing. Holly could only see the back of his head. 'The school is your flagship project, but the William Scrivener brand is there to be exploited.'

'Well, we brand stationery and calendars, you know,

sweatshirts, ties. Things like that.'

'Larry, Larry, Larry. What century are we in? Think outside the box.'

'Filofaxes?' ventured the principal.

'Think mobile-phone covers, polyphonic rings, baseball caps, skinny-fit T-shirts,' cried the man, turning round and smiling at Holly.

'Ladbroke,' said Holly.

It was Ladbroke Blake, the private detective that Holly had befriended after her dad's big-haired wife had hired him to follow her.

She had only left the message on his answering machine yesterday. She hadn't expected him to come so quickly. She didn't know what his plan was, but he was obviously using a false name because the principal looked quizzically at her and said, 'Ladbroke? Surely you recognise your godfather, Holly, Mr Somerset Oglander.'

'Excuse us,' Ladbroke grinned. 'It's an old family joke.' He held his arms out and said, 'Holly, how are you?'

Holly hugged him.

'I see,' said the principal. 'Well, I must say, Holly, your godfather has a lot of interesting ideas on the subject of schooling.'

'My ideas are nothing next to your achievements,' said Ladbroke.

'Oh, well,' said the principal, unable to hide his glee. 'I can't take all of the credit. The school has a long and noble tradition of educating the nation's finest and wealthiest children.'

'Modesty. I'll have none of it,' said Ladbroke. 'I recently returned from a tour of the top-ranking private schools in the USA and I have to say yours stands shoulder to shoulder with the best of them.'

'America,' said Principal Palmer, eyes wide. 'You're too kind.'

'But I have not come all this way simply to admire your wonderful school.'

'Yes, of course,' said the principal, fixing Holly with a serious look in his eyes. 'Now, Holly, please listen to your godfather.'

'Yes, Holly, I am afraid I have been sent here by your father, who is terribly busy campaigning in the election. I understand that you have been having some difficulty settling down.'

Holly looked down at her feet.

'Are you unhappy here?'

'No, sir,' she said quietly.

'You realise most children would give their right

kidney to come to this school?'

'Yes,' said Holly.

'I want you to promise me that you will stop all this misbehaving and try to settle in. Your father can't afford any scandal at this stage in his career.'

Ladbroke was holding her hands, and, as he said this, he gave them a gentle squeeze, which Holly took as a sign to demonstrate her acting skills, so she covered her eyes and began to sob.

'There, there,' said Ladbroke. 'Do you promise to be a good girl?'

'Yes, sir,' she replied.

'Your father is very proud of you,' said Ladbroke. To the principal he said, 'And I'll tell Malcolm what good hands she is in. Your security is second to none. Explain to me how these remarkable wristbands work again.'

'They're made of a plasticised metal which was developed by NASA for use in space,' said Principal Palmer. 'Nothing can cut through them. They allow the students to come and go as they please within designated hours and they are all fitted with short-range locating devices, preventing any repeat of last year's unfortunate incident.'

'The kidnapping.' Ladbroke nodded. 'Did they ever find out who was behind it?'

'No. Probably some local nut who realised he was in too deep, so released the boy.'

'Well, they are remarkable devices. Holly, let me see yours.' She noticed him slip his hand into his jacket pocket before taking her wrist. 'NASA, you say?' he said, inspecting the band.

'Oh yes, it is an advantage of having such generous sponsors of the school that we can always afford the best.'

'Hold on, what's this?' said Ladbroke, suddenly sounding alarmed.

Holly looked at her wrist and saw that, around the band, her skin looked red and sore. It didn't hurt, but it looked like it did. Ever so subtly, Ladbroke winked at her and she withdrew her arm.

'It's nothing,' she said, playing along.

'Let me see,' he demanded.

Holly reluctantly offered up her arm again.

'What is it?' said Principal Palmer.

'How long have you had this rash?' asked Ladbroke.

'Only since I've been wearing the wristband,' she replied. 'It's nothing.'

The principal walked round the desk and inspected the newly appeared rash. 'Holly, you should have said something.'

'What do you think is causing it?' said Ladbroke.

'Well, they did say that in some rare cases the wrist-bands might cause an allergic reaction.'

'Really? How fascinating.'

'Why didn't you tell me about this?' Palmer asked Holly, clearly embarrassed.

'I didn't want to make a fuss,' answered Holly.

'Didn't want to make a fuss? Don't be so silly,' said the principal. 'Don't worry. I'll call security immediately and have it removed. You don't mind carrying it with you instead, do you?' he asked.

Holly looked down at her pretend rash, and allowed herself a very small smile. 'No,' she said. 'I don't mind carrying it with me instead.'

After a security guard had been called and the wrist-band removed, Principal Palmer allowed Holly to accompany her godfather to his car, before returning to her lessons. Ladbroke put on his coat and wide-brimmed hat and followed Holly down the corridor

'What's your plan when you get out?' he asked quietly.

'Dirk's in the forest,' said Holly.

'The dragon?'

Although Ladbroke had never formally met Dirk he had had the pleasure of being knocked out by him. 'I've got to get back to London. Are you sure you'll be OK?' he asked.

'I know where Dirk is hiding so I should be able to find him.'

'OK, try to be safe.'

Ladbroke threw his hat into the back seat of his car, a grey Mercedes with a white stripe across the side, and drove away.

Chapter Thirteen

Holly spent the rest of the afternoon plotting her escape. She was told off three times for not listening and was almost caught out when, during art, Mr Learmonth caught her drawing a plan of the school grounds instead of the bowl of fruit in front of her. Luckily, Holly's drawing wasn't all that good and he seemed satisfied with her explanation that it was an artistic impression of the fruit.

By the end of the school day the plan was ready, but she needed help.

In the common room she found Moji sitting with some other prefects, flicking through glossy magazines, laughing at the problem pages.

'Hi,' said Holly, standing in front of her.

'Hey, it's Steve McQueen,' said Moji, making her friends laugh. 'How's it going, Steve?'

'Can I talk to you in private?' asked Holly.

'Sounds serious,' said Moji smiling, but she put down her magazine and followed Holly out of the common room. Holly led her out of the main door, to avoid being overheard.

'I need your help,' she said. 'I need to get out. I can't tell you why, but I've got a plan. This isn't a stupid running-away-from-school thing. It's important. I'll only be gone a few days.'

Moji looked at her. She could tell she was serious. 'Are you in trouble?' she asked.

'No, but someone is, and I need to get out to help him. You have to trust me.'

'Sorry, Holly. I already told you, my escaping days are behind me. I can't help you.'

'Yes, you can,' pleaded Holly. 'You're the only one who can. You're the best, Moji. You know this place better than anyone. I can't do it without you.'

'But even if you got past the fence, they'll find you because of the non-removable . . .'

'Wristband?' Holly interrupted, pulling it out of a pocket.

Moji sighed. She looked at Holly, so stubborn and strong-willed. It was crazy to help her escape but, looking into the girl's determined brown eyes, she was reminded of herself at that age.

'OK, Hol,' she said eventually, 'but I must need my head seeing to. What's the plan?'

Later that night, with Petal murmuring something about Versace in her sleep, Holly crept out of the room, dressed all in black. She slipped across the corridor to the cupboard, pulled a balaclava over her head and put on her trainers, then snuck to the main door, clinging to the shadows, where Moji was waiting for her, also dressed in black.

Without a word, Moji held her wristband up to the door and pushed it open. Holly darted through, swiftly followed by Moji. Outside, they took cover behind the two large pot plants. They stayed hidden for two minutes exactly, without speaking, then Moji nodded at Holly. Holly raised her thumb and Moji ran across the concourse in the direction of the football pitch.

Holly waited another minute before running to the tall conifer tree. She climbed up the tree, then across to the next, heading, tree to tree, along the path towards the main gate.

Reaching the final tree she climbed down to a lower branch so that she could see the security cabin. The light was on. At this time of night there would be two guards in the cabin, the patrolling guard having just got back from his round. The cold penetrated Holly's clothes. She shivered and blew into her hands to keep warm. She checked her watch. If Moji was on schedule, the alarm light would be flashing inside the cabin right about now.

Sure enough, the door opened and a guard hurried out. Holly stayed still, focused on the task. Another few minutes passed then a second guard left the cabin.

Holly waited for another minute, giving Moji enough time to make another hole in the fence, flushing out any extra guards on duty tonight. No one else appeared, so she jumped down from the tree and approached the cabin cautiously, but before she could get too close, she heard a dog barking and a voice say, 'What is it, Bruno, boy? Is there someone out there?'

Holly ran to the nearest tree and scrambled up it, grazing her hands and knees in her desperation to get away. The door opened and Hamish appeared, holding the barking poodle on his leash. Holly's heart thumped like it was trying to get out. Bruno dragged the large man to the tree where she was hiding. This was it, she thought, she would be seen for sure. She shrunk back into a shadow and shut her eyes in case they gave her away in the darkness.

'What you barking about, you daft poodle, Bruno?' she heard the guard say, standing directly below her.

His walkie-talkie crackled and a voice from it said, 'Hamish, you need to come and check this out. They're springing up everywhere.'

'Aye, I'm coming,' said Hamish, waving a torch in Holly's direction and then saying, 'Come on, Bruno, there's no one there. Ah wish you'd bark a bit more opportunely.'

Holly opened her eyes to see the guard disappearing down the path, dragging the hysterical poodle behind him.

She jumped down and darted into the open cabin. The high-tech control panel was alive with lights, indicating that Moji had successfully made a series of holes around the perimeter fence. Only one of the holes was big enough for anyone to fit through, way over behind the main building, but Holly wasn't leaving through a hole in the fence.

She found the override for the cameras and made those overlooking the main entrance point in the opposite direction then pressed the button that opened the front gate. She grabbed her bag, ran full pelt through the gate and pulled it shut behind her.

She had done it. She was out.

Soon the guards would find the wristband by the large hole, assume she had discarded it during the escape, and search for her in the wrong direction. It would take them hours to realise they had been tricked. By that time, Holly should have reached Dirk.

She headed through the dense undergrowth, deep into the forest in the direction of the caves where Dirk said he was hiding out, but it was dark and it was difficult to stick to a straight line. She stumbled over twisted roots and slipped on clayey ground.

After several hours without any sign of Dirk or the caves, it began to rain. Moisture seeped through the fabric of her trainers, dampening her feet. An unforgiving wind cut through the trees, making her shiver.

She tried to hum a tune in her head to lighten her spirits, but her teeth were chattering too violently. She was freezing. Her nose felt like it was made of ice and she could no longer feel her toes at all. She tried to avoid the muddy lower ground, using roots and vines to scramble up banks but, with no light, kept stumbling into puddles. Muddy water squelched over the tops of her trainers.

She felt scared. Leafless branches hung down like giant claws, catching and scratching her face. Unseen animals scurried away as she disturbed them. Strange sounds filled the air. The trees rustled and creaked. She never knew a forest could make so much noise.

She stopped and listened. She could hear voices. At first she thought it was her imagination, but they grew nearer. She pushed herself into the shadow of a giant oak tree and kept still. Two raspy female voices were arguing.

'If the manuman has served his purpose, why can't we schmunch him?'

'Because Vainclaw says so. It's all part of the plan, Salix.'

Holly struggled to see who was speaking.

'But what is this plan of his, Acer? I want action. Remember the old days when we used to terrofear entire villages for fun.'

'It's not like that any more. We can't let the manu-mans know of our existence until we know we can win the war, that's what Vainclaw says. They have weapons that would kill you in an instantesance.'

Holly could make out two dragons. They were thinner than Dirk and looked like two leafless trees skulking through the forest, getting closer to where she was hiding. Their heads were like twisted tree branches, with dark rough bark and cold green eyes. Thin lines of dirty brown smoke curled from their nostrils. One of them snapped its jaws at the other, causing the other to do the same. They were so close now that Holly could see rows of jagged moss-stained teeth.

'Well, I preferred it the old way. I can't bear all this schnooking around.'

'Sh!' urged the other. 'I can hear something breathing.'

Holly held her breath. The Tree Dragon stared into the shadow. It was looking directly at her. She had nowhere to run, so she shut her eyes tight, pushing herself against the tree, desperately trying not to move a muscle.

She could feel the dragon's hot sulphurous breath against her cheek. Holly felt sick with fear.

'There's no one there, Salix. No manuman would be this far into the forest so late,' said Acer.

'You never know with them. They get everywhere.'

The voices moved away. Holly opened her eyes. The dragons were walking away, swinging their heads to and fro as they moved, their long tails twisting behind them.

'You shouldn't be so scared of the pathetic creatures.

We're Kinghorns. Let's schumch the old manuman.'

The last thing Holly heard Salix say was, 'You stidiotical fool. You want to end up being banished?'

With the dragons gone, Holly stepped out of the shadow and tried to get her bearings. She was utterly lost, cold, wet and completely terrified. It took all her strength to hold back her tears. Holly didn't like to cry. Crying brought back sad memories of her mum, who used to cry all the time. The only time she had ever seen her dad cry was at Mum's funeral.

Holly sniffed and wiped her eyes, but the feeling was too strong. She dropped her head into her hands.

'I thought you didn't cry for real,' said a familiar voice.

She turned to see two friendly yellow eyes. It was Dirk. She threw her arms around his neck and now they were tears of relief that streamed down her face.

'Dirk,' she exclaimed. 'I was so frightened.'

Dirk brushed the girl's cheek gently. 'You don't need to be scared now,' he said kindly before adding, 'Come on, get on, they're getting away.'

Chapter Fourteen

With Holly on his back Dirk spread his wings and took after the two Tree Dragons, being careful to avoid being seen. Holly noticed that his wounds had completely healed over.

'Why aren't you at school?' he asked.

'There's a boy in my year, Callum Thackley, he's the Prime Minister's son and he was kidnapped last year and I think it was these Tree Dragons because he talks about creatures that look like trees. Then during band rehearsal . . .'

'You're in a band?' interrupted Dirk.

'It was an escape plan,' replied Holly. 'But these men in dark glasses came to the school, saying they were from the government and taking him to a photo call, but Callum screamed and yelled that they were coming for him. Why would he scream if that's all it was?'

Dirk looked doubtfully at Holly. It sounded ludicrous, but he had learned to trust her and he knew these Tree Dragons were up to something. Besides, the Prime Minister's son was exactly the sort of target he would expect the Kinghorns to go for, weak enough to overcome, but with enough power to prove useful. He already knew that Vainclaw employed humans to do his dirty work, from the two stupid crooks and Professor Rosenfield, so it was possible that the men in black did work for him.

'Quiet now, we're getting near,' he said.

In the early morning light Holly could see five Tree Dragons prowling around a clearing in the forest, heads bowed low. She tightened her grip on Dirk's neck.

Dirk landed silently behind a large fallen tree trunk and brought his wings to his side. He lifted his head to see the dragons. Something metallic glinted in the middle of the clearing.

The Tree Dragon Acer Campestre spoke.

'What is it? Why are we doing things we don't comprestand?'

'Strush up, Acer,' said Betula. 'Vainclaw has toldered

us to guard it. That's all you need to know.'

'What for, Betula? We don't even know what it is,' said Acer, breaking the circle and approaching the silver case in the centre of the clearing.

'It's the professor's case,' whispered Dirk to Holly.

The other Tree Dragons turned to face Acer and hissed at her.

'Stay away from it,' said Tilia.

'Yes, Acer, don't be stidiotical,' said Salix.

'It's some kind of manuman schmunching machine. We should master it ourselves,' said Acer, sniffing at the case.

'She's right,' said Buxus. 'Why wait for Vainclaw to come and steal all the glory.'

'Vainclaw is our master,' asserted Betula. 'He will lead us to victory against the manumans.'

Acer reached out her claws and tapped around the side of the case.

'You'll break it,' said Tilia.

Acer's claw must have found a button because the case slowly opened, revealing a computer screen set into the top. It flickered to life and the computer made a loud beep, causing the five dragons to jump back, allowing Dirk and Holly to see the screen. It read:

ROG Project
QC3000
NAPOW TECHNOLOGY
IDENTIFICATION REQUIRED
60 SECONDS BEFORE TIME-OUT

A red handprint appeared on the screen under the words and the voice counted down the seconds.

'What does it mean?' asked Buxus.

'I don't know,' said Acer. 'Shall I touch it?'

55 SECONDS
54 SECONDS
53 SECONDS

'If you don't stop I'll tell Vainclaw,' said Betula.

'If you do I'll schmunch you,' snarled Acer, reaching a claw to the screen and touching the handprint, which disappeared. The machine stopped counting down and said:

PROCESSING

After a few seconds a red cross flashed on screen along with the words:

INCORRECT INDENTIFICATION
MACHINE SHUTTING DOWN

As automatically as it had opened, the lid closed again.

'You've broken it,' said Tilia.

'I'll try again,' said Acer, trying to stop the lid from closing, but as she did so she screamed, suddenly pulling away her claw again.

'What happened?' asked Buxus.

'It bit me,' said Acer.

The lid closed. Betula stepped forward. 'From now on I'm looking after this,' she said, going to grab it in her mouth, but screeching and jumping back.

This time Dirk noticed the spark that flew from the case.

'It's giving off electric shocks,' he whispered to Holly.

'You stidiotical fool,' said Salix, 'We'll all end up in Euphorbia Falls for this.'

'I'm not scared of the Dragnet,' said Acer.

'Well, I am. We'll be banished to the Inner Core. That new Dragnet captain is arresting hundreds of suspected Kinghorns.'

'Vainclaw said we shouldn't worry about the Dragnet,' said Betula. 'Now, get back into guarding position. Enough of this. That includes you, Acer. You've done enough damage for one day. You better hope you haven't broken it.'

The Tree Dragons resumed their circling motion, swinging their heads from side to side.

'I've seen enough,' said Dirk, turning and crawling away. Once he was out of sight of the Tree Dragons, he leapt into the air, taking Holly up through the trees, bursting out of the dappled shadows into the full sunshine above the forest.

Holly allowed herself a small squeal of excitement. Flying over the trees was even better than jumping over rooftops. It was brilliant to be back with Dirk. She felt safe on his back, like no one could harm her. And special, like no one else in the world could be happier than she was at that moment in time. She thought of Petal Moses, who got everything she ever wanted, but she didn't have a dragon for a friend.

'I've missed you,' said Holly.

'Me too, kiddo,' admitted Dirk.

'How's Willow?'

'She's fine. Mrs Klingerflim's looking after her while I'm away.'

'Is that safe? She thought she was a dog last time she saw her.'

'That would explain why she keeps throwing sticks for her to fetch in the back garden and trying to train her to fetch the paper.'

Holly laughed. 'Where are we going?' she asked.

'That silver case is some kind of weapon. I want to know what it does,' replied Dirk, sailing down towards the black-and-white cottage in the middle of the forest. He landed quietly behind the stone wall and ducked down. 'This is where they've been keeping the professor.'

Holly climbed off his back and they approached a window in the cottage.

Looking in, Dirk said, 'It's empty,' and quickly moved to the front of the building and ducked through the door.

Holly followed him in and shut the door behind them.

She glanced around at the tatty furniture, coated in a thin layer of grime. 'What a dump.'

'Quick, I'll check this room, you look in the bedroom,' said Dirk, lifting up the worn cushions of the mouse-eaten armchair. 'We shouldn't stay here too long.'

'What are we looking for?' asked Holly.

'Clues.'

Holly found the bedroom through a door on the right. It was small and dingy, with a tiny window. She sat down on the bed and picked up a newspaper with yesterday's date on it. Seeing the picture on the front she shouted, 'Dirk, come and look at this.'

'What is it?' Dirk's head appeared around the door frame.

'I guess I was wrong about Callum,' she replied, holding up the paper. It was a picture of the Prime Minister and his family outside Number 10 Downing Street. His other two grown-up sons were smiling. Callum stood in front of his father, glaring fearfully at the camera. 'The men who took Callum must have been for real,' said Holly.

'Let me see that.' The room was so small that Holly had to stand on the bed so Dirk could get in as well.

'I'm not sure this room was designed for a drag—'

She stopped mid-sentence, interrupted by the sound of a car engine. Holly and Dirk looked at each other. The engine cut out and doors opened.

'Well, professor, as usual it has been truly gratifying indulging in such weighty discourse. Once again, apologies for my colleague's windy interruptions,' said the voice of the crook Arthur.

'Yeah, sorry about that. The fish pie I had last night keeps disagreeing with me gut,' said Reg.

'When can I go home?' asked the professor.

The front door opened.

'Mr G has requested that you remain here for the time being in case your services are required.'

'But I've reprogrammed the machine now. There's nothing more I can do.'

'You could put the kettle on,' said Reg. 'I'm parched.'

'Quick, through the window,' whispered Dirk, urgently lifting up Holly, pushing the window open with his tail and putting her through it.

'But they'll see you,' protested Holly. 'Even if you blend they'll walk straight into you in such a small room.'

Dirk placed her down on the ground and said, 'Don't worry about me, just run into the woods as fast as you can, wait five minutes, then come back, but make sure you get out of earshot.'

'What are you doing?' said Holly. 'They'll see you.'

'Don't argue, run.'

She jumped over the stone wall and ran full pelt into the woods as Dirk had told her, but before she got far she felt her feet slow down. She could hear music. Beautiful music. Her feet felt like lead, unable or

126

unwilling to take her any further from the sound. It was beautiful, like an ancient hymn sung in a forgotten language, like nothing she had ever heard and yet like it was coming from inside her, the harmonies and melody being produced by her own breathing. All she wanted was to hear the music, to get lost in it, to be the music.

Chapter Fifteen

irk found Holly standing on one leg, the other angled out in front of her, frozen mid-stride. Her arms were outstretched, her lips curled into a smile, her eyes open with a faraway look as though remembering a happy but distant memory.

'Rats of the wild frontier,' he cursed.

He zipped around her, lifted his paw to her face, said, 'Sorry, Holly,' and slapped her hard on her cheek.

Holly toppled to the side, waking from her stupor. 'What did you do that for?' she said, regaining her balance.

'Sorry, kiddo. The only way out of the trance is a jolt to the head. I tried to go as easy as I could.'

'What happened to me?'

'You heard Dragonsong.'

'Yes,' said Holly, the light returning to her eyes, 'it was beautiful. Like . . . Like . . . Like no music I've ever heard.'

'Well, I'm sorry.'

'Why are you sorry? It was amazing.'

'Come on, I'll show you.'

They approached the cottage. A yellow car was parked outside. As they went through the front door, Dirk said, 'Try not to scream.'

Holly stopped in the doorway. In front of her were the two crooks. Reg was sitting at the table. Arthur was standing by the doorway. A man with a bald head, who she guessed was the professor, was leaning over the cooker with a box of matches in one hand and a match in the other, as though about to light the hob. All three of them wore the same vacant look on their faces, standing perfectly still, like a moment preserved in time.

'Don't worry, I turned off the gas,' said Dirk.

'Is that what happened to me?' asked Holly.

'Yes. You heard the music right up to the point that I slapped you, didn't you?'

'Yes.'

'I only sang for a few seconds. It gets inside you.'

'It was almost like I was making it,' said Holly, smiling at the memory. 'Do they know we're here?'

'They can see the world around them, but they're not looking at it, and they'll only listen when spoken to directly. All they care about is the Dragonsong.' Dirk turned to the professor and said, 'Professor Rosenfield, I want you to stand upright and light that match.'

Instantly Rosenfield did exactly as Dirk told him.

'Wow. Can you make him do anything?'

'Yes. I could make him blow out the match or light the hob and make us all a nice cup of tea . . .'

'That's brilliant.'

'Or I could make him drop it and burn down the cottage with him and these two in it.'

Holly blew out the match. 'You could make him kill?'

'Lots of good dragons have died this way,' said Dirk. 'Dragonsong is a gift in the right hands, but a deadly weapon in the wrong. It's been against our laws to use it as a weapon for thousands of years. I hate it. I'd never have used it at all but I had no choice, I couldn't let them see me.'

'What do we do with them now?' asked Holly.

'We'll send them home after we've extracted information from the professor. Needless to say, these two idiots don't know anything.' Dirk turned to the professor and said, 'Professor Rosenfield, why are you here?'

Still smiling, with a spaced-out look on his face Rosenfield replied, 'I've reprogrammed the QC3000.'

'That's what it said on the screen of the silver case,' said Holly.

'What's it for?' asked Dirk. 'Is it a weapon?'

'It's a weapon, all right.' The professor smiled.

'Have you stolen it?'

'Yes, don't tell anyone, will you?' He spoke like a little child who had done something naughty and didn't want to get told off.

'Won't someone be looking for it, then?'

'No. Hardly anyone knows about it. It's top secret.'

'What does it do?' asked Holly.

The professor didn't answer.

'He'll only answer the questions or take orders from the first voice he hears,' said Dirk, turning to the professor and repeating the question. 'What does it do, professor?'

'It uses sonar signals to create small but significant movements in the earth's tectonic plates. It's completely revolutionary, the only one in the world.'

Holly gasped. 'It makes earthquakes.'

Dirk looked at her. 'So you have been listening in school?'

'No, I read it somewhere. The earth is made up of tectonic plates. They're always moving, but earthquakes are caused when they suddenly shift.'

'Manmade earthquakes,' said Dirk. 'Professor, what does AOG stand for?'

'Acts of God, weapons designed to create natural disasters like tornadoes, tsunamis and earthquakes so that governments can wipe out entire cities without having to declare war.'

'That's awful,' said Holly.

'That's humans,' said Dirk.

'It's dragons who have stolen it,' replied Holly.

'Fair point,' admitted Dirk, then to the professor asked, 'Who are you working for?'

'I don't know who they are. I've never seen the man with the deep voice. The only people I've met are the two silly idiots with the smelly car.'

Holly looked at Arthur and Reg, who remained oblivious to this insult.

'Where are they planning to attack?'

'I entered the coordinates but I don't know where

they relate to. I don't want to know. I don't want to be responsible.'

'I see, so if an earthquake happens, you can just convince yourself it was a natural one and you'll never know for sure if it was you.'

The professor nodded then added, 'But they can't make it work. I told them that.'

'Why can't they make it work?'

'It can only be activated by one person.'

'Which person?'

'It was developed for the British government. Only the Prime Minister of Great Britain can operate it,' said the professor, swaying a little. 'I told them, I can't get around it. It's programmed only to respond to his DNA.'

'Callum,' said Holly.

'Would it work with his son's DNA?' asked Dirk.

'No, it requires a direct match and it scans for exact fingerprints. Only the Prime Minister's hand will activate the machine.'

'What happens when the wrong person tries to operate it?'

'It shuts down and becomes impossible to touch for one hour.'

Holly could tell from the amount of white smoke coming from Dirk's nostrils that he was getting angry. 'And what did you get for your hand in all this, professor?' he asked. 'What does it cost to make you betray your country and your species, to break the law and put your job and your family on the line?'

The professor's distant smile neared. He leaned forward and whispered, 'Proof.'

'Proof? Proof of what?'

'Dragons. I saw a dragon once, while holidaying in Wales as a child. My parents said I was making up stories, of course, but I know what I saw and ever since then it's been an obsession of mine. My wife has never understood it and my colleagues laugh at me behind my back, but now they will have to believe me,' he said. 'Now I have proof.'

'What proof?' said Dirk calmly.

'Behind the TV. There's a parcel.'

Holly dived to the TV and pulled out the parcel. She placed it on the kitchen table, opened it up and lifted out what looked like a piece of ivory.

'A dragon claw,' said Dirk.

'A dragon claw,' repeated the professor.

'If only he knew who he was talking to,' said Holly.

Dirk took the claw from Holly and said, 'Professor Rosenfield, I want you to listen very carefully to me.'

The professor nodded and leaned forward.

'When I say, these men will take you back to the station. Catch a train home, go back to your wife, whom you love very much, and try to lead a normal boring life. You won't remember any of this conversation or the events of the last few days and when your wife asks, you'll say the cryptozoological conference was a complete bore and gradually, over time, your interest in dragons will wane. You'll find a new hobby. Holly, what's a good hobby?'

'Skydiving?' suggested Holly.

'Something safe.'

'Bungee jumping?'

'You'll become interested in stamp collecting instead, professor.'

'I'll become interested in stamp collecting,' repeated the professor.

Dirk turned to the crooks.

'You two, take the professor back to the train station. When you get there slap him in the face then slap each other.' He leaned forward and muttered something in their ears that Holly couldn't quite hear.

'What did you tell them?' she asked.

'I told Reg to drive carefully. Remember, they can see the world around them if instructed to look. He'll drive more attentively than he's ever done before.'

Compliantly, all three of them left the cottage and climbed into the car. Holly and Dirk followed them out.

'Will it work?' asked Holly.

'Dragonsong is very powerful, particularly on human minds, which are weaker than dragons. No offence.'

He tucked the claw in a fold of skin behind his right wing, motioned for Holly to climb on his back and they took to the sky.

'Where are we going?' she asked.

'I'm taking you back to school,' replied Dirk.

He tilted his wings to gain a little height. In the distance he could see the school. Holly saw it too.

'Why can't I stay with you?' she said.

He dipped down again, flying close to the tree tops.

'I'm sorry, Holly,' he said. 'I wish I could, but I can't protect you where I'm going.'

Dirk was telling the truth. He really did want to take Holly with him. On the whole, dragons were solitary creatures. Sometimes small groups would stick together for short periods of time if they had a mutual goal, like the Tree Dragons in the forest or the other Kinghorns he had encountered on his last case, but these unions would rarely last more than a few months. Dragons learned loneliness when they were abandoned as younglings. Dirk remembered the morning he awoke to find his mother gone. Barely ten years old, he had searched everywhere for her until, eventually, he realised she was not coming back. He only ever saw her once after that and by then it was too late. She was dead.

Maybe Dirk had spent too much time surrounded by humans, with their constant need for company, and perhaps some of that neediness had rubbed off on him because, since meeting Holly, he had come to enjoy having someone to confide in.

Chapter Sixteen

Dirk landed by the trunk of a large, fallen sycamore tree, near the perimeter fence of the school. Holly could see the main gate. She didn't want to go back. She wanted to stay with Dirk.

'Where are you going?' asked Holly.

'Those Tree Dragons said the Dragnet were arresting Kinghorns. That means they know something. I want to find out what. I've got to go and speak to the Captain of Dragnet and tell him what I know.'

'What's the Dragnet?'

'It's the Dragon Council's police force. Dragnet officers are Drab-Nosed Drakes, flightless, soil-eating dragons with a bad case of wing envy, but they're tough. If they saw you with me, I'd be banished and you'd be killed.'

'I could keep watch over those Tree Dragons while you're gone,' suggested Holly.

'Holly, you saw what they did to me. Besides, they don't even know what they're involved in. I need to get to the dragon behind all this.'

'You mean Vainclaw Grandin?' said Holly, remembering the name.

'Exactly.' Dirk sat with his back against the trunk, eyeing the surrounding trees, looking out for green eyes.

'If the Kinghorns want a war why would they choose a weapon which makes it look like a natural disaster?' asked Holly.

'I don't know. Maybe they're looking to weaken the human armies before the main attack. They're gaining in numbers but I doubt Vainclaw has a big enough army yet to take on the whole of humanity. He needs more supporters and the Council will never sanction war.'

'I don't want to go back,' protested Holly. 'I want to come with you, to help stop the war.'

Dirk craned his neck and looked her in the eyes. 'I'll come and see you as soon as I'm back, but I can't take you with me. I can't risk losing you.'

Holly could tell there was no way she would be able to persuade him. Quietly she said, 'OK. I'll go, but you have to promise to come back.'

'I promise,' said Dirk and he stood up and held out his paw, which Holly took and held to her cheek.

'Wait five minutes before leaving,' she said. 'I'll draw the guard away from the main gate, so you don't get seen.'

'Take care, kiddo,' said Dirk, 'and stay out of trouble.'

'Trouble?' smiled Holly. 'Me? Never.'

She hugged him one more time and ran into the woods.

Dirk sat back down and considered the case. It was the second time he had found himself up against the Kinghorns and yet he was still no closer to Vainclaw Grandin. All he knew was what Karnataka had told him, that Vainclaw was a Mountain Dragon, that he was cautious, smart and extremely dangerous and that at the great conference he claimed to be the first in the air, voting to declare war on humanity.

Deciding that enough time had lapsed, Dirk stood up and stretched. He spread his wings, flapped them a couple of times, and took to the sky.

Flying south over the forest, towards the caves, Dirk

felt almost like Holly was still with him. It was like when you've been wearing a hat all day and then take it off but it feels like you're still wearing it; Dirk could almost feel her arms around his neck, and her body pressed against his back. He looked over his shoulder to make sure, but she wasn't there. Of course she wasn't. She was back at school, probably making some poor teacher's life a misery. He supposed that this was what it was like to miss someone.

He glided towards the base of the hill, making sure there was no one around. For human visitors the caves weren't very exciting, being neither very big nor particularly deep. There were no cave paintings to boast of nor any spectacular stalactites or stalagmites to marvel at.

Certain there was no one around, Dirk swooped down and landed inside one of the caves. If you had told one of the few human visitors that the shallow caves provided an entrance to a matrix of tunnels deep inside the bowels of the earth, they would probably have thought you were mad or being silly, or just plain lying. Humans considered rock to be a very solid, non-communicative substance.

Dirk, on the other hand, knew that rock was actually quite malleable and, although not the world's greatest conversationalist it was, at least, capable of understanding and following simple instructions, providing they were spoken in the ancient language of Dragonspeak and said very slowly.

Dragonspeak was a beautiful language but it was dated and lacked the richness and subtleties of, say, English or French, which was why dragons tended to use human language when talking to each other. Rock, on the other hand, had resolutely refused to learn a new language in all the billions of years it had been hanging around.

Dirk crouched down on a slab of stone and made a strange growling, muttering noise, syncopated by clicks and barks, which roughly translated meant, 'Down, please.'

The rock shifted with ease, lowering Dirk into the ground like an organic elevator. His head disappeared beneath the surface and the rock re-formed above him, cutting out the daylight and plunging him into darkness.

After several hours descending through the dark, it grew lighter and Dirk felt the surface he was standing on pull away from under his feet. He braced himself. Orange light appeared beneath his claws and he dropped down into a vast tunnel, landing heavily and feeling a twinge in his back like something kicking against it. He looked over his shoulder. At first he saw nothing and then he noticed the faint outline of a girl, barely detectable, but there if you looked for it, blended to match his red scaly back.

'Holly?' he said disbelievingly. 'But how?'

A pair of brown eyes appeared.

'Hi, Dirk.' Holly's mouth materialised.

'I don't understand . . .' he started. 'You can . . . You can blend like me . . . even your clothes. How are you doing that?'

'I don't know. At first I thought that hiding from the security guard during my escape was lucky but when that Tree Dragon looked straight at me in the forest and didn't see me I began to realise what was happening. I was doing it without thinking. Like you said, you just have to think like whatever you're trying to blend with. It's easy, really, isn't it?'

'It's easy for Mountain Dragons. It's not supposed to be easy for humans,' countered Dirk angrily.

'I thought you would feel me on your back when I climbed on.'

'The skin on my back is pretty tough. I suppose that's why you asked me to wait five minutes before leaving the clearing, giving you time to sneak back on.'

Holly nodded. 'But how come I can do it?'

'I don't know,' he replied, confused. 'Unless . . .'

'What?' she asked.

'Knights used to drink dragon blood to steal their powers.'

'Yuck,' exclaimed Holly. 'I haven't been drinking your blood. That's disgusting.'

'When I came to the school I was still injured. Some of my blood had rubbed on to your shin. You put it to your tongue to see what it was.'

'Would that be enough to do it?'

'It would seem so, wouldn't it.'

Holly glanced around at the tunnel. 'What is this place anyway?' she asked.

'We're just off the north-western arm of the lithosphere tunnel.'

'Where does the light come from? I can't see any lamps.'

'This is earthlight.'

'Earthlight?'

'The Inner Core gives off light and heat. It's where dragons get their energy, just like humans can't live without the sun. That's why we cast shadows upwards. The nearer you get to it, the lighter it grows.'

Holly gazed up at Dirk's shadow. 'It's amazing,' she

said. 'I'm probably the only human ever to have been here.'

Dirk smiled. He would never have admitted it but deep down he was pleased she was with him.

'Hey, Mountain Dragon, what are you doing?' called a voice.

'Quick, blend,' ordered Dirk. Holly imagined she was made out of the same red scaly skin as Dirk's back and her body changed colour to match it.

A dirt-brown creature appeared round the corner. It had a large belly, a long droopy nose and a dark metal chain attached to its short tail, with a heavy-duty neck cuff held in its hand. In the other hand was a burger-shaped lump of mud. It waddled forward, sniffed the mud burger then nibbled it and grunted approvingly.

'Identify yourself and your purpose.'

As he spoke tiny bits of mud flew out of his mouth.

Dirk wiped his face. 'My name's Dirk Dilly and I want you to take me to see the Captain of Dragnet,' he said.

The Drake puffed out its chest, showing its metal Dragnet badge. 'I'll do no such thing. I don't know what the world's coming to, civilians ordering Dragnet officers around. I never could have believed it. In my day, dragons showed a bit of respect.'

Dirk hated Dragnet officers. Drakes went into the

145

Dragnet for one reason. Power. They were smaller than dragons but the neck cuffs they carried enabled them to capture and arrest even the largest dragon. They were stupid, petty-minded and corrupt and they were normally looking for what they could get out of any given situation.

'All right, what will it take to persuade you?' asked Dirk.

'How dare you?' said the officer indignantly. 'Are you attempting to bribe a Dragnet officer?'

'What's your name, Drake?'

'You are addressing Officer Balti Grunling, six hundred and thirty-two years wearing the badge.'

'Well, Balti, I'm sure there's something I can get to persuade you.'

'Dragnet officers do not take back-handers. I would cuff you for suggesting it, except I've got this mud burger on the go.'

Dirk waited, saying nothing.

Balti lifted the unappetising burger and opened his mouth to bite, but stopped. 'There is one thing I'd like,' he said quietly.

Dirk smiled. 'What's your poison?' he asked.

Balti pulled out a small glass pot. He lifted it up with careful reverence and whispered, 'Pepper.'

Chapter Seventeen

'Pepper?' exclaimed Dirk.

'Dust of the gods.' Balti showed him the old pepper pot. 'Can you imagine what it's like eating soil all your life?'

'Lacking in variation?' ventured Dirk.

'It's so boring. What's for breakfast? Soil. Fancy a spot of lunch? That'll be soil, then. Dinner? Soil. Midnight snack? Soil. Soil soil soil. Then I discovered pepper. It doesn't half liven up a meal. This one's running out though.' Balti shook the pot. It was almost empty.

'Well, Officer Grunling, you're in luck,' said Dirk, smiling. 'As it happens I'm rather well connected in the condiment world. Obviously, I don't have any on me, but take me to your captain and I'll bring you more pepper than you can dream of: black pepper, white pepper, garlic pepper, Sergeant Pepper and his Lonely Hearts Club Band. And not just pepper. How about some mustard?'

'Mustard? What's that?'

'Oh, you'll love it. English, French, Dijon. I'll bring you a selection.'

Balti's small piggy eyes darted around as though concerned someone might be watching, then extended his paw and said, 'OK, it's a deal, Mountain Dragon. This way.'

Dirk followed Balti down the corridor.

'Why do you want to meet the captain?' asked the Drake.

'I want to ask him what he knows about the Kinghorns.'

'Oh, he knows lots about that lot. Since becoming captain he's made hundreds of arrests. He's cleaning up this place.'

For Holly, clinging to Dirk's back, trying to keep still enough to stay blended, it seemed like ages until eventually Balti stopped at a dark iron door and said, 'All right, Mountain lad, we're here.'

'Where's here?' asked Dirk.

Balti banged on the door.

'Euphorbia Falls Prison,' he said as the door opened. They entered an enormous cave and Holly marvelled at the scene in front of her. They stood on a wide path that circled an expansive underground lake which must have been over a mile wide. On the far side of the cave was a huge waterfall. It was making the water choppy and tumultuous. In the middle of the lake was a round island with six large, rocky mounds.

Rough, craggy walls sloped up from the path at a steep angle. The cave reminded Holly of the inside of an amphitheatre she had once visited while on holiday in Greece, but ten times as big, and instead of seats for spectators, the walls were lined with dark metal-barred doors, and rather than sunburnt tourists taking photos, the path around the lake was lined with Dragnet officers, some dirt brown like Balti, others different shades of grey or dull greens, all staring across the water at the island.

'Wait here, we're in time for a trial,' said Balti excitedly, shuffling to the edge of the path.

Dirk moved backwards, away from the Drakes.

'What's going on?' Holly whispered in his ear, being careful to keep her head as still as possible when she spoke to prevent it from reappearing.

149

'This is a prison. These cells are full of dragons await-ing trial.' Dirk spoke out of the side of his mouth.

Holly looked up and saw hundreds of eyes, some yellow, some green, a few red, staring out from behind the cell doors.

'Are all these prisoners Kinghorns?' she asked.

'I don't know. I can't believe Vainclaw has so many followers, but they must have done something to get arrested.'

The Drakes jostled each other, standing shoulder to shoulder at the water's edge.

'What are they doing?' asked Holly.

'Trying to get a good view,' replied Dirk. 'This is a rare occasion. The six councillors are wise but they're extremely old so it's difficult to get them all in one place for long enough to conduct a trial. One of them normally wanders off before they get anywhere.'

'What councillors?' asked Holly.

'On the island.'

Holly looked more carefully at what she had mistaken for six rocky hills. They were dragons, each one the size of a house. Their stony grey skin was pitted and textured like wax solidified on the side of a candle. They lay perfectly still, with white smoke billowing from their huge nostrils, then one opened its mouth, revealing rows of teeth like huge stalactites and stalagmites.

Holly could just about make out two smaller dragons standing in front of the councillors. One of them spoke into a voice projector like the one Karnataka used to scare off visitors. The sound filled the cave.

'The Council calls Almaz Bartosz, Sea Dragon accused of Kinghorn collusion.'

In response, one of the Dragnet officers in front of them turned round and scampered up the sloping wall to a cell door, unlocking the latch and opening it.

From within the cell appeared a rather scared-looking female Sea Dragon. She glanced about the cave, then spread her wings and flew to the island in the centre of the lake.

His job done, the Dragnet officer jumped back on to the path and pushed his way back to a spot by the water's edge.

'The Council calls Salt Sheasby, Sea Dragon, as witness against Almaz Bartosz,' said the voice.

A second Sea Dragon entered the cave through the waterfall, gliding down to the island, where she addressed the Council.

'What's happening?' said Holly. With the sound of the waterfall echoing around the cave and the chattering of the Drakes, it was impossible to hear anything from the island other than the dragon with the voice projector.

'It's like a human court, but without any lawyers. The Council will hear witnesses and then make their decision,' replied Dirk.

Again, the voice filled the cave. 'Any dragon wishing to speak in defence of Almaz Bartosz should appear before the Council now or forever be silent.'

Holly looked to the waterfall but no dragon appeared.

'Isn't anyone going to defend her?' she asked.

'Most dragons live alone, far away from each other as well as from humans. Many don't have anyone to defend them,' said Dirk.

The voice spoke again. 'Then, councillors, make your decision.'

The six enormous councillors lowered their heads.

'Are they discussing the case?' asked Holly.

'In a way,' replied Dirk. 'The councillors long since gave up speaking. They think to each other.'

'They can read each other's minds?'

'It's more like listening to each other's minds, but essentially, yes.'

The white smoke that issued from the councillors'

nostrils turned black and the voice boomed, 'Almaz Bartosz, found guilty of Kinghorn collusion.'

The crowd of Drakes along the path cheered and jangled their metal chains happily.

The Sea Dragon, Almaz Bartosz began to sink down, as though being swallowed by the island.

'What's happening to her?' asked Holly.

'The rock is taking her to the Inner Core.'

'But it wasn't fair. No one defended her,' said Holly.

'Keep your voice down,' replied Dirk sternly.

'Psst, Mountain Dragon.' This voice came from behind them.

Dirk turned round and looked up at a cell door a few metres above him. A brown nose poked through the bars and two dirty yellow eyes peered down.

'Dirk Dilly, it is you.'

Holly couldn't turn her head without reappearing but she recognised the high-pitched whine as Karnataka, the liquorice-loving Shade-Hugger who lived under London.

'Karny, finally behind bars where you belong,' said Dirk.

'Come on, Dirk, give me a break. I've been set up. I've been accused of Kinghorn collusion. Me,' he squeaked. 'You've got to help me. My trial's up next.

This new captain of Dragnet is arresting dragons on flimsy evidence. Look at all these dragons. If Vainclaw had that many Kinghorns he would already have declared war. And you know what the Council's like. If no one defends you they assume you must be guilty. Remember what happened to Elsinor.'

No one had defended Karnataka's brother, Elsinor, when he had been accused of breaching the forbidden divide, not even Karnataka himself.

'Give it up, Karny, I know you sold your claw to the professor.'

'I don't know what you're talking about,' protested Karnataka.

'Come off it. Are you saying it wasn't you that knocked me out in that old hospital in London?'

'Knocked you out? Hospital? London?' Karnataka's voice got so high pitched that it was virtually ultrasonic. 'The last time I went above ground I almost got killed for the sake of some human baby.'

'I'm not a baby,' blurted Holly, forgetting herself.

'Who's that?' said Karnataka, pushing his nose as far through the bars as it would go, trying to get a better view.

'I didn't hear anything,' said Dirk. 'Shut up,' he muttered to Holly, through his teeth.

'It's that girl, isn't it?' said Karnataka excitedly. 'Why can't I see her?'

'You shut up too,' growled Dirk. Bringing a human this far into the dragon world wasn't just breaking the law. It was smashing, slicing and serving it on a plate.

'Who are you talking to?' demanded Officer Balti Grunling, turning round to address him.

'No one,' replied Dirk.

'He's talking to me,' said Karnataka. 'He's going to testify on my behalf.'

Balti looked up then back down at Dirk. 'No talking to prisoners.'

The voice from the centre of the cave rang out again. 'The Council calls to trial Karnataka Cuddlums, Shade-Hugger, accused of breaching the forbidden divide, stealing and selling dragon parts to humans.'

Dirk laughed.

'I'm about to be banished to the Inner Core for a crime I didn't commit and you're laughing,' said Karnataka. 'What's so funny?'

'Cuddlums,' Dirk chuckled.

Chapter Eighteen

Once again, the sonorous voice echoed around the cave.

'The Council calls the witness against Karnataka Cuddlums, Grendel Sheving, Shade-Hugger.'

A second brown-backed Shade-Hugger appeared through the waterfall, shook himself dry and flew down to the large island.

'What is it?' said Holly quietly, seeing Dirk's ears prick up.

'It's Karny's cousin,' muttered Dirk, 'I met him at Karnataka's place.'

They watched as Grendel made his statement to the Council and then the voice spoke again.

'Any dragon wishing to speak in defence of Karnataka Cuddlums should appear before the Council now or forever be silent.'

'Hold tight,' murmured Dirk, spreading his wings. 'Things might get dangerous when I land, so I'll give you time to get off and hide as close to the edge of the island as possible. Stay hidden no matter what happens. OK?'

'OK,' replied Holly, clinging tightly as Dirk flew over the Drakes, across the expanse of water.

'How is all this connected with the professor and the Tree Dragons?' she asked.

'The professor was given a Shade-Hugger claw as evidence of dragon existence. And you don't just find dragon claws lying about the place. Why do you think no human has ever found one? Anyone dealing in dragon parts has most probably just lopped off their own.'

'That's disgusting,' said Holly.

As they grew nearer, she realised how huge the six councillor dragons were. Since meeting Dirk, all the dragons she had seen were around the same size as him, but the councillors were like mountains in comparison. Great clouds drifted from their nostrils like smoke from industrial chimneys. Their mouths were big enough to stand inside, each tooth was bigger than Holly, and their yellow eyes were like vast windows.

One reared up, but a dark metal chain around his neck kept him in place.

'They're chained down,' Holly whispered in Dirk's ear.

'It must be to stop them wandering off. Remember, these dragons are so old that they used to keep dinosaurs as pets.'

Dirk circled the island. In front of the enormous councillors were the two Shade-Huggers standing on elevated stone slabs and two yellow-backed Scavenger dragons. Holly recognised them immediately.

'It's the Kinghorns,' she said, remembering with a cold shiver her encounter with them by the Thames.

'Yes, the yellow-backed Scavenger brothers, Leon and Mali. It's bad news if these two are in charge,' said Dirk.

Mali, the smaller of the two Scavengers, held a chain between his teeth, the other end of which was wrapped around Karnataka's neck. His brother, Leon, stood by the cone-shaped voice projector. They both scowled at Dirk as he landed at the edge of the island and reared up on to his hind legs with his wings outstretched, giving Holly enough time to jump off and dive to the ground without being seen.

'My name is Dirk Dilly. I am here to testify in defence of Karnataka . . .' He paused and smiled at Karny. 'Cuddlums.'

Leon turned round, snarling angrily, 'You!'

'It's that detective,' said Mali, holding the chain with his claws.

'Arrest him, Captain Leon,' demanded Grendel.

'Don't order me about, Shade-Hugger,' snarled Leon, turning on Grendel.

'So you're the Dragnet captain that's been arresting half of the dragon kingdom,' said Dirk.

'Councillors, this dragon is a traitor,' pronounced Leon.

WE WILL HEAR HIS EVIDENCE.

Holly heard the words clearly in her head and somehow knew that they had come from the councillors even though none had opened its mouth to speak. 'Councillors,' pleaded Leon, 'this Mountain Dragon moves amongst humans. He should stand on trial, not as a witness.'

IS THIS TRUE? asked the councillors soundlessly.

'Please hear me, before you judge me,' said Dirk. 'What I have to say affects every dragon in this great chamber and every dragon in the world.'

'Yow shouldn't listen to this silly Mountain Dragon,'

said Grendel. 'I'm the key witness in this trial. I already told yow, Karnataka sold a claw to a human.'

'Then why are you the one with a missing claw?' said Dirk, leaping on to Grendel's back, grabbing his back left paw and holding it up in the air. 'And don't call me silly,' he growled in his ear.

The councillors' huge eyes fell on Grendel's damaged foot.

'You were limping when I saw you back at Karnataka's place,' Dirk said to Grendel.

'It's not true.' Grendel struggled beneath Dirk's weight. 'I lost my claw years ago in an accident.'

'Well, I've good news, then, Cinderella, because I've found it,' said Dirk, pulling out the claw he had tucked behind his wing and holding it up.

'Where did you get that?' demanded Grendel.

'I found it in the hands of a human,' replied Dirk, 'the human you sold it to.'

'Councillors, don't listen to him. I told yow, it was Karnataka,' protested Grendel. 'He sold it to the professor.'

'I never mentioned a professor,' replied Dirk. 'And I suppose it was you who attacked me back at the old hospital.'

'Give me that,' exclaimed Grendel, trying to grab the

claw, but unable to escape from Dirk's firm grip.

'You mutilated yourself for the Kinghorns and then you set up your own cousin, didn't you? What for, Grendel? Surely not just so you could move into his garish bachelor pad?'

'Watch what you're calling garish,' interrupted Karnataka.

'Come on, the flaming columns are a bit over the top,' said Dirk. 'What's Vainclaw got planned, Grendel?'

'I don't know anything about it,' he screamed.

'You're another one of Vainclaw's cronies, aren't you?'

'I'm not.'

'You're a Kinghorn. Admit it.'

'I'm not a Kinghorn, I just did it for the gold,' blurted out Grendel. 'Oops.'

'Got you,' announced Dirk triumphantly, jumping off Grendel's back. 'Councillors, you've heard this Shade-Hugger's confession. How do you find Grendel Sheving in the matter of selling his own body parts to humans?'

The councillors shut their enormous eyelids, remaining utterly still for a moment. The white smoke from their nostrils turned black and their eyes opened again.

WE FIND GRENDEL SHEVING GUILTY OF BREACHING THE FORBIDDEN DIVIDE.

'No,' screamed Grendel angrily, flapping his wings trying to escape. But the stone beneath his feet had already formed over his claws and was dragging him down into the ground. 'Please, Dirk. Have mercy. I spared your life back at the hospital. I could have killed you but I didn't.'

'We were in the middle of London. Even if you'd had the guts to kill me, you'd never have been able to dispose of my body without being seen.'

The stone speedily pulled Grendel down.

'Please, have pity. I can't be banished,' he pleaded, his head now level with the ground. 'I've got sensitive skin. I'll get a rash.'

'For the last time, what's Vainclaw plotting?' insisted Dirk.

'I don't know. I don't know anything.'

'Then send me a postcard. I hear the Inner Core is nice and toasty this time of year.'

Grendel screamed and wriggled to get free but there was no stopping the rock as it formed over his head, silencing his desperate cries.

Chapter Nineteen

Leon turned and addressed the councillors.

'Councillors, please,' he begged, 'the fact that this Mountain Dragon has the claw is enough to convict him.'

The councillors looked at Dirk.

WHAT DO YOU SAY, MOUNTAIN DRAGON?

'If I hadn't retrieved the claw it would have led to the exposure of our kind. This is what your captain wants. He works for Vainclaw Grandin. He and his brother are Kinghorns.'

'Lies,' barked Leon, sending a line of fire at Dirk.

Dirk dodged the flames, but Leon jumped forward and swiped at him with his outstretched claws. Dirk ducked then leapt into the air, spinning round and whacking Leon with his tail.

Leon rolled over and shouted, 'I could do with some help, ar' kid.'

Mali let go of the chain holding Karnataka and dived at Dirk, but Dirk jumped out of the way.

'Don't worry, councillors,' said Leon. 'Me and ar' kid will have this one locked up in no time.'

The councillors remained still and silent.

Holly watched helplessly as the two Scavengers surrounded Dirk, circling menacingly, sending sporadic bursts of fire at him.

In a sudden movement, they both pounced forward. Dirk tried to bat them off, but they were too quick for him. Mali landed on his back and pinned him down with a claw to his mouth, to stop him breathing fire.

'Councillors, I am going to burn this traitor's eyes out as an example to all Kinghorn spies,' Leon roared, sending fire from his mouth, and walked slowly towards Dirk.

Holly wished there was something she could do but to reappear would be death to them both. Then she noticed Karnataka, slowly backing away towards the edge of the island.

Dirk could feel the heat on his face from Leon's fire.

It wasn't dying that he minded. It was leaving Holly alone in this place. He struggled, desperate to get free, but Mali held him down firmly.

Then he felt the weight lift from his back and he sprang up on to all fours to see Karnataka wrestling Mali to the ground.

Dirk leapt into the air and came down hard on Leon's back, taking him by surprise, getting him in a firm headlock and hauling him back across the island, thrashing wildly. He held him from behind, flattening his pointy yellow ears against his head and digging his claws into his chin.

'Still fighting Vainclaw's fights for him?' said Dirk.

Swiping his tail and struggling to get free, Leon replied, speaking in a low whisper, 'The Kinghorns' time is near, Mr Detective. Soon Vainclaw will lead us to victory.'

'These dragons in the cells are all innocent, aren't they, Leon?'

'Of course,' hissed Leon. 'You think we'd arrest our own kind? It doesn't take much to accuse an innocent dragon. How do you think I got rid of my predecessor as captain?'

'And you're not worried about being found out?' replied Dirk.

'The Drakes follow my orders and these senile councillors wouldn't know a real Kinghorn if he smacked them in their big stupid faces,' replied Leon triumphantly.

'I think they might now,' said Dirk, releasing him and allowing him to see that he had dragged him all the way across the island to the voice projector, holding his mouth by the thin end of the cone, broadcasting every word around the hall.

Dirk tapped the device and then spoke into it. 'Did everyone get that?'

Leon glanced back at the Drakes, who were waving their chains in the air and shouting, 'Traitor . . . Kinghorn scum . . . Arrest the scavengers . . . Betrayal . . .'

'You just said that to the whole cave, bro,' said Mali.

'I think it may be time to go, ar' kid,' he replied.

Mali, who had wrestled himself free from Karnataka, nodded. 'Last one out is a pot-bellied cave dweller.'

WE HAVE BEEN TRICKED. THIS CAPTAIN IS A TRAITOR.

The six councillors reared up and tried to snatch the Scavengers out of the air, but the chains that held them were too tight.

'You'll get what's coming to you soon enough, councillors. The time of the Kinghorns is near,' goaded

Leon. The Scavengers disappeared through the water-fall, pursued on foot by a squadron of angry Dragnet officers.

Dirk edged his way to where Holly was hiding and spread his wings again, giving her enough time to scramble back on and vanish from sight. He approached Karnataka and said, 'Thanks for your help.'

'Don't thank me. Thank your friend,' replied the Shade-Hugger, looking at Dirk's back, where Holly was hiding.

'Whatever you say, cuddly-tums.' Dirk grinned.

'This is why I don't tell anyone my surname,' sighed Karnataka.

'No, I think it's nice,' Dirk chuckled. 'Cuddle-bum-bums.'

Holly stifled a giggle.

'All right, very funny.' Karny sounded annoyed. 'Just don't spread it around, OK? I've got a reputation to think about.'

Dirk addressed the councillors. 'Councillors, as you now know, the Kinghorns have returned. You must release all these prisoners. The only real Kinghorns just flew through that waterfall.'

The councillors gazed at Dirk with huge sad eyes.

WE ALLOWED THE CAPTAIN TO CHAIN US

HERE FOR THE TRIALS, BUT NOW WE ARE TRAPPED. YOU MUST HELP RELEASE US.

'I have to return above ground,' said Dirk. 'I believe the Kinghorns are planning an attack on humans. I'm sure Karnataka will be more than happy to lend a claw to your predicament.'

THE KINGHORNS SHOULD BE STOPPED. THE SHADE-HUGGER WILL HELP US.

'Me?' said Karnataka, backing away. 'Thanks, guys, but I've got to get back to my pad.'

THE COUNCIL ELECTS KARNATAKA ACTING CAPTAIN OF DRAGNET.

'Seriously, no . . . I . . .' Karnataka stopped mid-flow. 'Captain? Captain Karnataka. Yes, I like the sound of that. All right. It's a deal. Does it come with a pension and health benefits?'

RELEASE THE PRISONERS, CAPTAIN, AND FIND A WAY OUT OF THESE CHAINS.

'Sure thing, see you around, Dirk. Make sure she makes good on her promise. The size of a torpedo, OK?' said Karnataka, taking to the air and flying over the lake to bark orders at the Drakes.

The councillors turned to Dirk.

THE WATER WILL TAKE YOU BACK.

'Hold tight,' muttered Dirk under his breath, taking

flight towards the enormous waterfall.

Holly felt fine spray dampen her face. 'What did they mean, "the water will take you back"?' she asked. 'Water flows down, not up.'

'Not when it's asked nicely it doesn't,' replied Dirk.

Holly saw the plummeting water pull away, like curtains being drawn, and Dirk flew into the gap, folding his wings and settling on a bed of water that formed beneath him, mid-air.

Holly couldn't believe her eyes.

She looked around, confused by what was happening, and saw that the water was circling them, swirling above her head. They were in the middle of a giant air bubble.

GOOD LUCK, MOUNTAIN DRAGON, thought the councillors.

Holly's stomach lurched as she and Dirk rose against the flow of the waterfall. The bubble took them to the top of the waterfall, then along an underground river.

'What's happening?' she said.

'The councillors have asked the water to take us up.'

'Dragons can talk to water?'

'You can talk to anything, just don't expect much conversation in return,' said Dirk.

It was an amazing sensation, rushing upwards inside

the sphere of water. The orange earthlight revealed a narrow tunnel, carved out over thousands of years by the underground stream. Stalactites hung down, occasionally so low so that they penetrated the bubble and almost hit Holly as they whizzed past.

'What did you say to Karny to make him help me?' asked Dirk.

'I told him that my dad works with the ministry of confectionery and hinted that I could get my hands on a piece of liquorice the size of a torpedo.'

Dirk laughed.

'How come I could hear the councillors?' she asked.

'Dragon thoughts get more and more powerful with age. The councillors are so old they don't have to speak at all any more. That's how they're able to speak to the water. Rock is easy enough to order around, but water takes a lot more persuasion. It's kind of fickle.'

'How long will the journey take?' asked Holly.

'A few hours. We're a long way down,' replied Dirk.

The movement of the water was smooth and the sound of the swishing liquid was strangely calming. Holly relaxed her grip on Dirk's neck. She felt exhaustion overtake her and it wasn't long before she drifted off to sleep, dreaming strange watery dreams.

Chapter Twenty

Holly didn't know how long she had been asleep when she was awoken by Dirk saying, 'Get ready. We'll take the rock from here.'

He leapt out of the bubble with a splash and landed on a stone. They must have been a lot nearer the surface because the earthlight had grown dim and dusky. Dirk said something in Dragonspeak and the rock lifted them up.

'Where are we going?' asked Holly.

'Back to the caves,' replied Dirk. 'I've got to find those Tree Dragons and stop them. I'm taking you back to school. No stowing away this time. It's too dangerous.'

'But . . .'

'No buts.' Dirk cut her off. 'I can't take any more risks. Those Tree Dragons are vicious and I can't always protect you.'

Holly protested but nothing she said would make Dirk change his mind. As they grew nearer to the surface, the earthlight ebbed away completely so that all Holly could see were Dirk's yellow eyes, blinking in the darkness.

Cracks of light appeared in the rock above them.

'We're almost there,' said Dirk. 'Close your eyes. The sun will hurt them after so much exposure to earth-light.'

Holly shut her eyes tightly. As they surfaced, she felt sunlight on her face and swirling red shapes appeared on the backs of her eyelids. She clamped her hands over them.

'Open them gradually,' said Dirk.

Using the palm of her hand as a visor, Holly blinked open her eyes. The sunlight hurt her eyeballs, but it felt good on her skin. The early morning sun was climbing up the blue sky. White fluffy clouds drifted by. The forest looked vivid and green and the air tasted fresh and pure. Holly felt glad to be above ground again.

After hugging and saying goodbye to Dirk by the

fallen sycamore tree, this time for real Holly walked quickly to the main gate, where she was greeted by the familiar sound of a barking poodle.

'Come back, have you?' said Hamish, typing in the security code to open the gate. 'D'you know the trouble you've caused?'

'How are you, Bruno boy?' asked Holly, patting the dog.

'Never mind him. Ah'm taking you to the principal's office.'

'What day is it?' asked Holly. The time underground had left her feeling disorientated.

'What sort of question is that? It's Thursday morning.'

Holly had made her escape on Tuesday night. She had only been away for one day. It felt like much longer.

In the reception area, the principal's secretary was very carefully painting each nail as a different national flag and was currently working on the rather tricky crescent moon in the Turkish flag, which she had decided to place on her thumb.

'Yes?' she said, not looking up.

'Ah've got the wee lass who ran away,' said Hamish.

The secretary looked briefly at Holly before returning

173

her full attention to her nails.

'The troublesome Holly Bigsby,' she said flatly. 'You'll have to wait.'

Holly sat down and Hamish reached into his pocket and pulled out an energy bar, which he proceeded to feed to Bruno.

Raised voices were coming from inside the principal's office.

'It is an absolute outrage. I tolerate the press, but TV . . . You've turned the concert into a media circus.'

It was Miss Gilfeather's voice. Holly remembered that today was the day of the school concert.

'Please, Vivian, think of the coverage. You can't buy publicity like this. I was thinking if it goes well we could release an album in time for Christmas. Diversify or die, as they say.'

'Whoever says such a thing? I am not interested in diversifying. It's a school concert in a local village hall, not a rock concert in Wembley Stadium.'

'It's just a few cameras. Everyone who is anyone will be there.'

'My musicians have enough pressure without inviting the world and his wife.'

'I've also said that Petal Moses can do a number,' said the principal nervously.

'Petal Moses!' Miss Gilfeather's voice exploded with such force that the secretary slipped and covered the flags of France, Germany and Italy with a disastrous yellow streak. 'That girl has as much musical talent as a baboon.'

'Now, Vivian . . .'

'If that.'

'But her mother's coming. What a coup. The press will have a field day. It'll be bigger than a royal wedding. Please, Vivian, I can't do it without your consent.'

There was a pause.

'Oh, all right, but I'm not happy,' said Miss Gilfeather at last. 'Now, I have to go. The coach is waiting.'

'Yes, thank you, Vivian. Thank you so much.'

The principal's door opened and Miss Gilfeather emerged, dressed every bit as immaculately as always. Her eyes descended on Holly.

'Holly Bigsby, third trumpet,' she said automatically.

'Hello, Miss Gilfeather,' said Holly.

'Why are you not on the coach?'

'Erm . . .'

The principal interrupted. 'This girl has run away from school. I will take care of her punishment,' asserted the principal.

'You'll do no such thing. She is in my band. Holly,

go and get your trumpet and get on the coach.'

'But, Viv . . . Miss Gilfeather . . .' protested Palmer.

'You may administer your punishment after our concert. Holly, the coach.'

'Yes, Miss Gilfeather,' said Holly, smiling at Principal Palmer.

Miss Gilfeather looked at Hamish, who was tapping the confused poodle on his nose, while quietly chanting incantations in his ear.

'What are you doing to that dog?' she demanded.

'Ah'm teaching him aggression. It's an old Native American war chant.'

'You know that he's a poodle?'

'Aye.'

'And you're flat,' she said, marching out of the room.

'This isn't the last you'll hear of this, young lady,' said Palmer to Holly. 'You've acted very irresponsibly.'

'OK,' said Holly, making her way quickly to her room.

Petal was lying in bed, reading a fashion magazine. 'Oh, hello, you're back, are you?' she said frostily.

'Morning, Petal,' replied Holly cheerily, quickly changing her clothes and grabbing her trumpet case. 'I hear you'll be doing a solo at the concert,' she said.

'My mother has written a track for me. I'll be singing

it,' Petal replied proudly.

'Brilliant. I'll remember to bring my ear plugs,' said Holly, quickly leaving before Petal could think of a good response.

Outside the front of the school building the last few band members were boarding the coach. There was an excited buzz as she climbed on. The pretty flautists were doing each other's hair while the trombonists were trying to rally everyone to sing along with 'There's no business like show business'.

Holly spotted Callum sitting on his own, staring out of the window. She took a seat next to him.

'Are you looking forward to the concert?' she asked.

'No. Stupid concert is just another photo opportunity for Father.'

'The Prime Minister is coming?' said Holly. For a moment she considered whether the Kinghorns could strike at the concert, but how could they? The place would be crawling with security. She wondered whether her own dad would be coming. She hadn't even told him about being in the band, but if there was an opportunity to be seen with the Prime Minister you could bet he would be there.

'Callum, the tree creatures you've seen. I think I've seen them too. They're Tree Dragons. They're not in your head,' said Holly.

Callum looked at her then turned away, smoothing down his black hair nervously.

'They're in my head,' he replied.

'They're not. They're real,' protested Holly.

'No, they're not. They're in Callum's head. The doctors say I can control them.'

Callum stared out of the window and hummed to block out her voice. He refused to speak for the rest of the journey.

Chapter Twenty-One

Little Hope Village Hall was empty when they arrived. Miss Gilfeather got them to put out rows of chairs before asking everyone to take their places on stage for rehearsals.

As the day progressed, more and more people came in and out of the hall. Holly saw Hamish the security guard arrive with Bruno the poodle. Police officers with thick bullet-proof jackets and machine guns entered and checked for any possible signs of terrorism. They were met by men in dark suits and sunglasses. Holly recognised them as the men who had taken Callum. She looked over to where Callum was sitting, but he was avoiding eye contact.

TV crews arrived with loud-mouthed directors, scruffy-looking cameramen and long-haired sound-men. They set up lights, did sound-checks and fixed speakers outside so that the hundreds of onlookers who were expected to turn up would be able to enjoy the concert too. Locals gathered to witness the excitement which had descended on their sleepy village.

There was so much commotion that at one stage Miss Gilfeather shouted at everyone in the hall to 'Please be quiet!' unless they were involved in the band practice. A policeman with a face like a bulldog and an extremely large machine gun stopped his conversation with a TV director and look sheepishly at his feet, like a naughty school boy.

During the breaks they all had to stay inside the hall for security reasons. Not that Holly minded. She no longer wanted to use the opportunity to escape. She just wanted to get through the concert without mess-ing up too badly.

At half past five they did one complete run-through, which was, everyone agreed, a total disaster, but Miss Gilfeather was positive and said that a bad rehearsal usually indicated a good performance. After that, she announced that there would be no more practice and everyone should save their lips for the performance.

She took them through the order of events, so they knew what to expect.

'You will file on and take your places on stage. We will open with the Gershwin medley and then the first solo performer will come on. During that performance you will sit very quietly and politely, until I come back on and lead you in the second number.'

'Who's the first solo performer?' asked a tuba player.

Miss Gilfeather checked her notes. 'Petal Moses,' she said, barely managing to hide her disdain.

'Who's accompanying her?' asked a flautist.

'She'll have . . . oh dear me . . . She will have that most tacky of things, a backing track. Regardless of this, please show respect during all solo performances and remember you will be visible to the audience and the television cameras.'

By the time everyone had changed into school uniforms and eaten as many of the sandwiches and crisps provided as their nervous stomachs would allow, it had grown dark outside and the audience had started to arrive. A red carpet had been laid at the front door and snap-happy paparazzi had gathered on either side of it, taking pictures of every parent that arrived, on the off chance that they were famous.

181

Holly and half of the other band members were crammed around the backstage door, peeking out at the main hall, either celebrity spotting or looking for their parents arriving in their best suits and evening dresses. If they were deemed important enough they were interviewed by a showbiz reporter in a red dress. If not, they were taken straight to their seats by school prefects.

Each time someone really important arrived, the red carpet erupted like a war zone, the photographers screaming at the celebrity to look at them, smile for the camera, show a bit of leg and so on. The biggest of these explosions was for Petal Moses and her superstar mother. Petal's mother had obviously decided to pick up Petal, so they could arrive together. After their interview with the reporter, Petal came backstage, while her mother was escorted to her seat by a very excited-looking Principal Palmer. Petal wore a black sequinned dress and shoes so shiny that Holly thought they could probably be seen from space.

Holly moved away from the door, not wanting to look like she was interested. Petal entered the room, glanced at the half-eaten sandwiches and crisp packets lying amongst the instrument cases, and pronounced, 'I was promised my own dressing room.'

Miss Gilfeather, who was wearing a smart black trouser suit and crisp white shirt, said, 'I believe they're building one for your ego next door, Petal.'

Petal glared angrily at the teacher and handed her a CD. 'This is my backing track,' she said.

Miss Gilfeather took the CD, holding it at arm's length, and handed it to the pupil behind her, who happened to be Callum, smoothing down his hair and looking nervy.

'Callum, dear,' she said, 'There's a CD machine at the back of the room attached to the PA system. Please could you put this object in it?'

'Yes, miss,' he replied.

Outside, the red carpet exploded with noise again, louder even than for Petal and her mother, and Holly knew that Callum's dad, the Prime Minister, must have just arrived. Everyone crowded around the door wanting to see, except for Callum, who crouched down by the stereo. Holly joined him.

'Are you nervous?' she asked.

'I don't get nervous about music. Music is calming.' Callum smoothed down his hair and pulled something out of his pockets. 'Look,' he said.

'What's that?' asked Holly.

'Ear plugs,' he replied, showing her two wax

earplugs, 'for Petal's song.'

Holly laughed. He was making jokes. That had to be a good sign.

Miss Gilfeather told everyone to quieten down and to line up, so Holly said good luck to Callum and took her place behind her fellow trumpeters, Julian and Sandy.

As she stepped into the harsh TV lights in front of the audience, Holly became strangely conscious of her body movements, as though walking was something she had just learned to do. She found her seat, pleased she wasn't at the front of the stage, and gazed into the sea of faces.

Principal Palmer sat in the front row, talking animatedly to Petal's famous mother. Beside her was the Prime Minister and, next to him, Holly's dad, holding hands with his big-haired wife.

Holly had never liked her dad's wife, with her large blonde hair and expensive shoes. She resented that she had moved in with them so soon after Holly's real mother had died, like she could somehow replace her. But seeing the two of them holding hands, while her dad chatted to the Prime Minister, she had a strange feeling that she hadn't felt in years. She realised that it wasn't just Dirk and Willow she had missed since being at the school. It was her home and her dad, and being part of a family.

Her dad spotted her, smiled and waved. Although Holly knew they had come for the photographers more than her, for a fleeting moment she felt like a normal kid with a normal family, playing in a normal school concert. It was a nice feeling. She waved back.

Miss Gilfeather raised her baton and everyone lifted their instruments. She smiled, counted them in, and they began.

To Holly's surprise, it sounded OK. The mistakes that seemed so disastrous in rehearsals didn't seem to matter now.

When the tune finished the audience burst into rapturous applause.

'Thank you,' said Miss Gilfeather into the microphone. 'Next, one of our pupils will give a solo performance. Please welcome, singing a song written by her mother, Petal Moses.'

The audience clapped and cheered and Holly didn't mind. It was such a good feeling to be part of something like this, that she didn't begrudge Petal her moment in the spotlight. Petal looked surprisingly nervous as she took the microphone from Miss Gilfeather and took her place in front of the stage.

Holly saw her mum mouth 'Good luck', and someone pressed play on the CD machine backstage.

Holly had never had much time for Petal's mother's music but, as the backing track began, she found herself transported by its beauty. It was amazing, captivating, lilting and gentle. It was organic, like it was taking its rhythm from her own heartbeat. She never wanted it to stop.

In fact, everyone was so entranced by the music that came through the speakers that no one seemed to notice that Petal didn't start singing. Not even Petal. No one cared. No one cared about anything any more, just that the magical music should never stop.

Chapter Twenty-Two

After leaving Holly at the school gates, while deciding where to head next, Dirk was disturbed by something moving in the trees. He crouched down, blended with the ground and watched. There was another movement and he noticed the Tree Dragon, Betula Pendula, halfway up a silver birch tree, her back disguised against its bark. Her long claws gripped the trunk. Her pale green eyes focused on the school.

The perimeter gates opened and a coach drove out. It indicated then turned right, heading towards Little Hope. Betula leapt to the next tree, then the next. She was following the coach. Dirk spread his wings and took chase, flying above the forest, keeping a safe distance to avoid being seen by either the coach or Betula.

The coach arrived at Little Hope and parked outside the village hall. Betula stopped short of the village, but Dirk flew over her and landed on the roof of a corner shop, instantly blending.

The children got off the coach and Dirk noticed Holly amongst them. Before he could consider getting any nearer, a police van rolled into the car park and four armed policemen got out of the back. Two took their places at the front and back doors, one went inside, and one went up through the building and stepped out on to the flat roof.

'Rats,' Dirk muttered to himself, 'now I'll never get nearer.'

Throughout the day, more security arrived. Serious-looking men in dark suits and sunglasses checked the area thoroughly, going into people's houses, on to their roofs. Dirk was forced to hide even further away from the village hall.

He listened to conversations between villagers to figure out what was going on.

'It's a lot of fuss over a school concert, if you ask me.'

'Oh, but what a school. All those celebrity parents in our little village.'

'It's a disgrace, this disruption. I had to queue half an hour for my Bovril and bacon in the shop, stuck behind all those rude people from the telly.'

'It's not every day that you get a chance to meet the Prime Minister, though, is it?'

'I heard that his son has never been the same since that kidnapping incident, gone funny in the head, they say. Poor kid.'

As the sun set and the sky darkened, more people arrived, parking their cars along the road, going into the hall, or crowding around the front. Policemen outside kept the crowds in order, occasionally shouting at them through loudhailers to get out of the road if a car was trying to get through. All of the villagers had gone to watch the celebrities arrive, or climbed out on to their roofs to get a better view. Even the pubs had shut. There was no way that Dirk could get any nearer without being seen. It was so frustrating. All he could see were the flashing lights of the paparazzi and the silhouette of the policeman on the village hall roof. They had placed speakers outside the hall but they were facing the other way, towards the car park, and the sound didn't carry as far as Dirk. He figured that the concert had started because the flashing lights calmed down.

Then they stopped altogether.

In fact, all movement stopped.

The silhouette of the policeman on the roof, which had been circling, no longer moved.

Cautiously, Dirk jumped to a nearer roof, then another. More figures stood in the darkness like statues. In the street, a policeman held a loudhailer up to his mouth, but his lips weren't moving.

'Dirk jumped down to the road and saw that the policeman had been in the middle of shouting at three boys, who looked like they were running away, except they weren't running anywhere. He approached the village hall and saw more people, all unmoving, wearing the same faraway look in their eyes that could only mean one thing.

Dragonsong.

Dirk heard voices coming from the car park and dived for cover at the side of the building. He moved quietly in the shadows and found himself face to face with a familiar figure. Wearing a wide-brimmed hat and a long overcoat, Ladbroke Blake stood, rooted to the spot. The last time Dirk had met Ladbroke he had knocked him out and nicked his hat and coat. In spite of this, Ladbroke had helped him when he was unconscious and, more importantly, kept his mouth shut about dragons. So it was with a whispered apology that Dirk lifted off his hat, poked two holes in the rim with his claws and placed it over his own head.

He moved into the crowd around the red carpet. Photographers stood frozen, holding up their cameras or cleaning their lenses. Autograph hunters held books and pens in the air and police stood in front of the rails. The voices grew nearer and Dirk lowered his head, looking through the holes in the hat.

'Thank you, manumans, oh, I feel so special. No photos, please. What's that, little manuman? You want my autograph? Why, of course.'

The Tree Dragon, Acer Campestre, reached out her long twig-like claws and pulled a book and pen from a little girl's hand, scribbled something in the book and placed it back. If she had been aware of this, the little girl would have screamed and cried and run away. As it was, she stared unknowingly into nothing.

'Don't be stidiotical,' said Betula Pendula, skulking behind her.

All five Tree Dragons were prowling up the red carpet, heads swinging from side to side, staring at the frozen humans. Two of the dragons held the silver case between them, the QC3000.

'Make sure you don't touch any of the manumans,' said Betula.

The Tree Dragons entered the building, walking straight past an armed policeman with a face like a bulldog. They slammed the door shut behind them.

Dirk spread his wings and jumped. Ladbroke's hat flew off and Dirk landed behind the static policeman on the roof. He opened a door in the roof, where a ladder led down past the rafters to the hall below. Dirk squeezed himself through the door and climbed down into the rafters, where he could see rows and rows of parents, sitting on wooden chairs, all enjoying the best concert they had ever heard, oblivious to the five Tree Dragons walking down the aisle between them, approaching the stage where the band sat. He picked out Holly, second row back, sitting under the spell of the Dragonsong, her trumpet across her lap.

A speaker next to his ear crackled, making him jump and almost lose grip of the rafter.

'Brothers Kinghorn, dragons true,' a voice appeared through the speakers. It was the same deep voice he had heard in the old hospital. 'I, Vainclaw Grandin, welcome you.'

Chapter Twenty-Three

On hearing the voice, Betula, Buxus, Tilia, Acer and Salix bowed their heads low, then Betula looked up and spoke.

'The first up-airer, Vainclaw Grandin, we humble bark sisters are humblonified by your presence. We didn't know you would be here personally.'

'I grow tired of being let down by inferior dragons, so have decided to oversee this mission myself,' replied the voice.

'We will not let you down, sir,' said Betula.

'You already have. You allowed the professor to escape.'

'The manuman disappeared while we were guarding the box.'

'You are idiots, but it is of no matter. He served his purpose.'

'What purpose? What does the manuman box do?'

'Yes,' agreed Acer. 'What are we doing?'

'You will know soon enough. Bring the case to the raised ground.'

Dirk watched Buxus and Tilia carry the silver case up the aisle, whispering as they passed under him.

'Why won't he come out?'

'The boss doesn't like to be seen,'

'Shouldn't we tell him about the Mountain Dragon?'

'Strush up. He'll be angrious if he knows we let him get away.'

They placed the case on the stage by the feet of the tall woman wearing a black trouser suit and holding a baton.

'Salix and Acer, keep watch at the door.' Vainclaw's voice continued barking out orders. 'Do not touch any of the humans. It doesn't take much to knock these feeble bipeds out of their stupors. Betula, stay by the case.'

The Tree Dragons stood guard, Salix and Acer by the door, Buxus and Tilia on either side of the stage and Betula in front, sniffing at a girl in a black dress with one hand held to her mouth as if miming holding a microphone.

'My voice was the first heard by all of these pathetic humans, which means that they will do whatever I tell them,' Vainclaw announced. 'Mister James Thackley, please stand up.'

A man in the front row, with greying hair and a smart suit, stood up. Dirk recognised him as the Prime Minister of Great Britain. To the left of the hall stood his personal security guard, trained to lay down his own life in the course of duty if necessary, and yet smiling vacantly, as the man he was paid to protect obeyed every command of the deep voice from the speakers.

'Approach the silver case on the stage, Prime Minister Thackley.'

The Prime Minister stepped forward.

'Do you recognise this device?'

The Prime Minister gazed uncaringly at the box and said, as though in his sleep, 'It's the QC3000. It's a weapon. I hope I never have to use it.'

A deep thunderous laugh came through the speakers and the Tree Dragons joined in, snapping their jaws together in appreciation.

'Quiet!' hollered Vainclaw.

Dirk had to do something to stop the Prime Minister from operating the machine. He could easily snap him out of his stupor with a whack from his tail, but to wake up the most powerful man in Britain in a room full of dragons would be as good as starting the ultimate war himself.

'Kinghorns, too long has our species hidden from mankind,' proclaimed Vainclaw. 'Too long have we cowered in corners, skulked in shadows, waiting for a disease to eradicate this pest from the face of the planet, or for them to blow themselves up with their own bombs. And why did we hide? Because we were too scared to fight. We should have destroyed these hairless apes the moment they climbed down from the trees. We should have killed them when they were still banging rocks together, trying to make fire. We, who breathe fire but are too afraid to use it. Soon, we will not be afraid and I will lead all dragonkind, united as Kinghorns, into war against these soft-skinned mammals.'

Throughout this oration, the soft-skinned mammals in the hall remained seated on their uncomfortable wooden chairs, the words flying past them like paper aeroplanes.

Dirk, meanwhile, had crept silently across the rafters, stopping directly above Holly. He retrieved Grendel's claw from where it was tucked behind his wing, held it above her head, took aim and, as Vainclaw's speech finished and the Tree Dragons cheered, he dropped it.

'Ow!' A sharp pain in Holly's skull shook her out of the beautiful trance.

For a moment she felt sad and lost without the music, then a voice, as deep as a well, cried, 'Silence'. She was disorientated but remained still and took in the scene in front of her. The Prime Minister was standing in front of the silver case on the stage.

By his side, a Tree Dragon looked up and said, 'What was that?'

'What?' replied the deep voice.

'There was a noisound from the raised ground, Vainclaw, sir.'

Holly froze. The Tree Dragon jumped on to the stage, standing on its back legs. Holly copied the looks on the faces of the other band members, smiling vaguely and staring at nothing, hoping the dragon couldn't see her shaking hands.

'Anyone awakious up here?' asked the dragon.

Holly kept her eyes fixed firmly in one spot.

'It's nothing,' said the Tree Dragon, jumping back down.

Holly breathed a controlled sigh of relief and noticed that lying on her lap next to the trumpet was the dragon claw. Moving her head as little, and as slowly as possible, she looked up and saw in the rafters two yellow eyes. Dirk's head appeared and then his paw, which he put to his mouth and acted like he was speaking into a microphone. He pointed to the back of the stage and repeated the mime.

'It's time for these short-life creatures to do what they do best and die,' continued Vainclaw's voice though the speakers.

Holly noticed that Petal's microphone had gone and realised what Dirk was trying to say. Vainclaw was using it. In order to flush him out, she had to cut the sound.

She gently placed her trumpet on the floor, slipped the claw into her pocket and dropped down to her knees. Being careful not to knock over the music stands, she crawled between the other band members, watching the movements of the Tree Dragons through the forest of legs. The plug socket was along the edge of the stage.

'Dragons will once again take their rightful place as rulers of the world,' continued Vainclaw.

Holly waited until the Tree Dragon swung its hideous head the other way, then made her move, lying flat on the stage floor and wriggling forward. The Tree Dragon looked back and she blended to avoid being seen. She felt its eyes on her. She could hear it breathing. She waited a couple of terrified seconds then opened one eye. It had turned away.

'And I, Vainclaw Grandin, the first up-airer, will . . .'

Holly reached forward over the side of the stage and flicked the socket off.

The voice cut out.

'What's happened?' shouted one of the Tree Dragons.

'I don't know,' said another.

Holly remained hidden as the backstage door was pushed open. Heavy grey smoke billowed out, as though the whole building was on fire. The smoke thinned a little as it filled the hall and Holly could see a Tree Dragon cowering fearfully in the corner. In the doorway, a shape shifted inside the smoke and two yellow eyes opened. Head first, a dragon stepped into the hall. It was a Mountain Dragon, like Dirk, but its underside was a deeper green, almost the colour of Dirk's blood, and its back was crimson red. It was larger than Dirk too and, as it passed, its tail seemed to go on for ever, snaking behind its body, swinging from side to side.

The Tree Dragons bowed their heads low and whispered reverently, 'Vainclaw Grandin . . . Master.'

'Get up, you fools,' snarled the dark Mountain Dragon. His head swung round and Holly could see his face, lean and angular, his eyes, sharp and predatory, grey smoke billowing uncontrollably from his flared nostrils. 'Boy, why does this voice projector device no longer work?'

The door opened again and a small dark figure stepped out of the backstage room, shaking with fear, smoothing down his greasy black hair. It was Callum. 'I . . . I . . . I . . . don't know,' he stammered. 'It could be a fuse or a . . .'

They were using Callum. Holly realised they must have forced him to switch Petal's backing track with the Dragonsong. He must have done it when Miss Gilfeather handed him the CD.

'Never mind,' snapped Vainclaw. 'I will finish this face to face. Come, boy, and watch your father at work.'

The Tree Dragons snapped their teeth at Callum, and he whimpered quietly, muttering, 'They're in my head . . . I can control them . . .'

He followed Vainclaw fearfully to the stage, where the Mountain Dragon lifted his head level with the Prime Minister's, inspecting him like a waxwork in a museum.

'Prime Minister Thackley,' he said. 'Open the QC3000.'

Chapter Twenty-Four

All five Tree Dragons had gathered around the silver case, their pale green eyes focused on the Prime Minister, fumbling to open it. Above them, Dirk watched from the rafters as Holly snuck back to her seat on stage, unseen.

'Finally, we will clasp mankind's precious technology in our claws and turn it against them,' said Vainclaw.

'How does it work, boss?' enquired Betula.

'Is it a bomb?' asked Tilia from the other side of the stage.

'Or a missile?' added Acer enthusiastically.

Vainclaw looked at the Tree Dragons disdainfully and growled, 'Just keep watch and stay quiet, Bark-backs.

You'll know soon enough.'

The Prime Minister must have found the switch because the case opened, its lid lifting automatically and words appearing on the screen, illuminating his blank, expressionless face. The machine spoke in a flat electronic voice:

ADG Project
QC3000
NAPOW TECHNOLOGY
ENTER DNA IDENTIFICATION
60 SECONDS BEFORE TIME-OUT

'Prime Minister Thackley, please raise your right hand,' said Vainclaw.

The Prime Minister obeyed.

'Boy, stand close and watch your father initiate the dawn of a new era.'

The Tree Dragons grunted approvingly, nudging the terrified-looking boy forward with their jagged noses. Dirk shifted in the rafters so that he was directly above and prepared to swipe the Prime Minister's hand away with his tail, but before he could act, Holly jumped up and ran to the front of the stage. She reached out her hand to stop the Prime Minister, only to find her way blocked by Callum.

'Callum,' she said, 'get out of the way.'

But Callum grabbed both her wrists and clamped her down against the stage floor.

'Do it,' he snarled, turning to Vainclaw. 'Make him do it.'

'Prime Minister,' said Vainclaw. 'Place your hand on the screen.'

The emotionless voice continued to count down:

45 SECONDS BEFORE TIME-OUT

The Prime Minister reached his hand towards the screen. Dirk swung his tail, knocking it away. The Kinghorns looked up in confusion as Dirk swiped his tail again, whacking Betula on the side of the head, sending her flying across the hall.

He dropped to the floor, and reared up on to his hind legs, claws drawn, ready to fight.

'Who is this? Get him, kill him,' ordered Vainclaw.

Acer flew at Dirk, but he ducked, whacked the back of her head and sent her crashing into the front row of the audience. Principal Palmer, Petal's mother, Holly's dad and his wife instantly awoke from their trances to find themselves underneath what seemed to be a rather angry tree with sharp teeth and claws. They screamed and it jumped off.

'The trees are attacking,' yelled Principal Palmer hysterically. 'Run for the door.'

Acer flew over their heads and landed in front of the door, snapping her teeth and hissing, 'Stay where you are, manumans.'

28 SECONDS BEFORE TIME-OUT

'Prime Minister, touch the screen!' said Vainclaw firmly.

Ducking an aerial assault from Tilia, Dirk succeeded in knocking the Prime Minister's hand away again, but this time Betula and Buxus came at him from behind and sunk their teeth into his tail and legs, dragging him to the floor.

'Prime Minister, are you all right?' shouted Holly's dad, clutching his wife protectively. 'What are these things?'

'They're d . . . dragons,' stammered his wife.

'Impossible,' said Principal Palmer. 'Dragons don't exist.'

'What would you call them? Kittens?' replied Petal's mum hysterically.

'Strush up, manumans,' snapped Acer. 'Or I'll flame-grill your faces.'

'Leave them, alone,' screamed Holly.

'Holly? Is that you?' barked her dad, unable to get past Salix and Tilia, who were now penning all four of them in.

'Stop wriggling,' spat Callum, his sweaty hands holding Holly down.

'Don't you understand, they want to kill us all,' she said desperately.

'They're in my head,' said Callum. 'They do what I say.'

'Petal was right in the first place. You are crazy,' said Holly, wrestling an arm free and sending her elbow hard into his face, pushing him off. Grabbing the silver case, she twisted it round so that the Prime Minister's hand hit the back of the lid.

6 SECONDS BEFORE TIME-OUT

Holly placed her palm on the screen.

PROCESSING DNA

'You stupid little girl,' snarled Vainclaw, swiping at her angrily and catching her leg with his razor-sharp claw.

Holly fell to the floor, screaming, clutching her leg, blood oozing through the gaps in her fingers.

'Holly,' yelled Dirk, but he was silenced by Betula's claw digging into his jaw.

'You filthy beast, that's my daughter,' shouted Holly's dad.

'Leave her alone,' screamed his wife, but Salix snapped wildly, preventing them from moving.

INCORRECT INDENTIFICATION
MACHINE SHUTTING DOWN

The lid began to close automatically.

'No!' shouted Callum, trying to stop it and receiving an electric shock.

Holly crawled over to Dirk, her leg throbbing in agony with every movement. Buxus and Betula stood on top of him, their claws and teeth digging into his skin. 'Get off him, you vile creatures,' she said.

'Do you know this girl?' demanded Vainclaw.

Callum wiped his bloody nose with his sleeve and smoothed down his dishevelled hair. 'Yes,

Mr Grandin, sir,' he said. 'The girl said she knew about those monsters . . .'

'We're Tree Dragons, manuman. Don't forget it,' growled Acer, approaching Callum threateningly.

'Leave him alone,' snapped Vainclaw. 'Don't worry, boy, they won't harm you while I'm here.'

'But how could she know? The monsters are in my head, not hers.'

'That's right, Callum,' purred Vainclaw. 'It's all in your head. Now, what's wrong with this machine?'

'The details I read in Father's folder said it takes an hour to reset if the wrong hand touches the screen.'

'Then we will wait,' announced Vainclaw. 'Your father is still in the trance.'

Callum turned to his father, who still had that distant look in his eyes, his right palm raised.

'Not so important now, are you, Father?' he spat, walking around him. 'Not too busy to ignore Callum.'

He turned to Vainclaw and said, 'Make him bow.'

'Bow down to your son, Prime Minister Thackley,' said Vainclaw. 'Kneel before your new master.'

Unquestioningly, the Prime Minister got down on to one knee.

'Callum Thackley, what are you doing?' demanded the principal.

'What have you done to my daughter?' shouted Holly's dad.

Petal's mother cried out, 'Please don't touch my precious Petal!'

'Your precious what?' snarled Vainclaw.

'This one,' said Callum, pointing at Petal.

'Well, that's one way to pass the time while we're waiting,' said Vainclaw, 'killing humans.'

'Let me do it,' said Acer.

'No, she's only a little girl,' screamed Petal's mother.

'Stay where you are, Acer,' ordered Vainclaw. He turned to address Petal's mother. 'I could kill your daughter the same way you could squash a fly.'

'Do it,' urged Callum. 'Kill her.'

'No,' shouted Holly, staggering up and limping between Vainclaw and Petal, feeling weak and dizzy from the loss of blood.

'Get out of the way,' said Callum. 'It's the way things work. Superior animals kill inferior ones. Just like Petal killed your mouse, my dragon will kill her, if I tell him to.'

'She doesn't deserve it.' Holly collapsed to the floor.

'Kill them both,' said Callum.

'The great Vainclaw Grandin takes orders from a human, does he?' muttered Dirk through his teeth, feeling Betula's claws dig further into his face.

'I follow no one's orders,' growled Vainclaw, whacking Callum over his head with his long serpentine tail. 'Never tell me what to do again, boy.'

Callum giggled nervously and smoothed down his ruffled hair.

Vainclaw looked at Dirk. 'I suppose you're the detective that the Scavengers told me of? Dirk Dilly, I believe? You do seem to like sticking your nose in other people's business.'

'I thought it was his nephew,' said Salix.

'Strush up,' replied Betula.

'As long your business involves trying to kill innocent humans, I'll be there to stop you,' said Dirk, Betula's claw piercing his skin with every syllable.

'Or at least here to watch me. The machine will be working again in one hour.'

'Where are you planning to attack this time, Vainclaw? London, again? New York? You'd better choose carefully. As soon as the machine is used, they'll shut it down. You'll only have one shot and it will take more than one earthquake to destroy mankind.'

'Destroy mankind?' Vainclaw said mockingly. 'What an outdated notion. I did used to believe that we should destroy mankind, but not now. Humans have proved themselves far too useful.' Vainclaw stroked the silver case and received an electric shock. He pulled his claw away quickly. 'Every human that survives the war will be put to work in weapons factories, gold mines and farms, to work for their masters. I'm not going to destroy mankind. I'm going to enslave it.'

'And what's your role in this, Callum?' said Holly, crawling across the floor to Dirk, leaving a trail of blood behind her.

'Humans will be slaves and Callum will be the slave master,' said Callum. 'Callum will be more important than Dad or Principal Palmer or Petal or you or anyone. It's all in my head. I control it.'

'No, it's not, Callum. This is real and you're helping them kill.'

'Enough,' said Vainclaw. 'Enough of this futile chit-chat.'

'Holly Bigsby! Callum Thackley! I demand to know what's going on?' shouted Principal Palmer from across the hall.

'Silence,' shouted Vainclaw. 'Everyone waits in silence until I say so. Bark-backs, watch the humans and the detective. Don't worry about the girl. She'll be dead soon.'

'Holly, are you OK?' called her father.

'No, Dad, I'm not.' She tried to shout but the words came out as a breathless whisper.

'Can't we schmunch one of them while we're waiting? Just a little one?' begged Acer.

'After we have activated the weapon you can have your fun, Acer,' replied Vainclaw, 'when you burn this building to the ground and everyone in it.'

Holly, close your eyes and sleep.

The words appeared in Holly's head. She felt tired and confused, but she knew by looking into his big yellow eyes that they came from Dirk.

Sleep, Holly, close your eyes and sleep.

Chapter Twenty-Five

For Principal Palmer, Petal's mother, Holly's dad and his wife, it had been like waking from a wonderful dream to find themselves trapped in a terrible nightmare. They sat huddled together, in the middle of the hall, holding hands in a circle, while the Tree Dragons watched them, their sharp teeth snapping every time they spoke or sobbed or tried to move.

For Principal Palmer, it was some consolation that one of the hands gripping his so tightly belonged to Petal Moses' extremely famous American mother.

'I thought your last album was very good,' he whispered.

'I hardly think this is the time, Palmer,' said Mr Bigsby.

'Strush up, manumans,' said Acer. 'Not a noisound, not a whelper, or I'll scrunch all of you.'

'Ow,' yelped Callum on the other side of the hall, withdrawing his hand from the silver case.

'Be patient, boy,' said Vainclaw. 'The hour is almost up.'

'Callum is tired of waiting,' replied Callum.

'Don't you think your fellow Kinghorns deserve to know who they'll be murdering with this human weapon?' muttered Dirk.

Vainclaw lowered his head and peered into his eyes. 'They know that they are furthering the Kinghorn cause. That's enough for my loyal followers.'

'Yes,' said Betula. 'We are not traitors to our species, like you.'

'Then why are you helping him slay dragons?' said Dirk.

'What's he talking about?' asked Buxus.

'Do you want to tell them or shall I?' he continued.

'We are only killing those who stand in our way,' replied Vainclaw calmly.

'You mean the manumans?' said Buxus.

'Humans will die, don't worry about that, Buxus,' said Vainclaw.

'That might be true, but they're not the target, are they?' said Dirk.

'Shall I kill him?' said Betula.

'No, I've heard lots about this Dirk Dilly, the dragon detective. I want to see how good a detective he really is.'

Betula eased her foot off a little, allowing Dirk to talk more easily.

'I was just lying here quietly bleeding to myself, trying to see the bigger picture, when everything came together: the professor, the boy, the weapon, the Shade-Hugger's claw, the Scavengers, and these charming Tree Dragons. The whole thing.'

'Go on,' said Vainclaw.

Dirk continued. 'Last year you ordered the kidnap of this poor defenceless child. These vicious Tree Dragons took the boy and scared him out of his wits.'

'That's not true,' said Callum. 'Mr Grandin saved me from the tree creatures.'

'That's what he made you think,' continued Dirk, looking at Vainclaw. 'You came to his rescue and promised to protect him if he agreed to work for you. You released him, but stayed in contact. With the doctors assuring him that you were a figment of his imagination, he no longer knew the difference between real and unreal. You had him working for you, rifling through his father's work? That's how you came to hear of the AOG Project.'

Vainclaw nodded. 'Very good, Mr Dilly. Most of the documents were boring or inconsequential things about hospitals and schools, but yes, he did manage to uncover some rather interesting items on weaponry.'

'You discovered that one of the top scientists working on the AOG project had a rather interesting weakness, an obsession with dragon mythology. You persuaded that snivelling Shade-Hugger, Grendel, to donate a claw as a bribe to the professor. But why install the Scavenger Leon as Captain of Dragnet?'

'Where's Holly?' said Callum, realising that she was no longer lying next to Dirk.

'Never mind the girl,' snapped Vainclaw. 'She's probably crawled off to die in some corner. 'Continue, detective. You really are quite good, aren't you?'

'In order to win a war against humans, you need an army. But the councillors would never allow that. They'd send the Dragnet to arrest you. The trials were just an excuse to keep the councillors chained in Euphorbia Falls, while you got the Prime Minister where you could manipulate him into operating the machine. As soon as that machine resets itself, you'll wipe out Euphorbia Falls, the Council and the whole of the Dragnet. You'll become the most famous dragon murderer since Saint George himself.'

Vainclaw opened his mouth and flames shot out, scorching Dirk's face and catching Betula's foot, causing her to scream and hiss in pain.

'Never mention that name in front of me,' Vainclaw shouted. 'I can see that watching all those late-night human detective shows has paid off, but you're wrong. I won't be famous at all. Earthquakes are natural disasters. It will look like an accident. In a couple of minutes the machine will work again, the Prime Minister will oblige us with his hand, and we will destroy Euphorbia Falls and half of Europe with it. And without the Council or the Dragnet to stop me, I will gather my army and begin the ultimate war against humanity.'

'It won't work. Your Scavengers revealed themselves as Kinghorns. The prisoners have been released. It won't take them long to find you.'

'It will take the Council weeks to get out of those chains,' said Vainclaw. 'They're as good as dead already. Soon all shall follow me.'

'What's that noise?' said Acer.

Someone was banging on the door.

'This is Officer Balti Grunling of Dragnet. We have reason to believe there is illegal Kinghorn activity within this building.' The amplified voice came from outside. 'Come out with your claws down and your mouths shut.'

'Impossible,' said Vainclaw. 'It is against Dragnet procedure to come this close to a human settlement.'

'Not when you've been illegally using Dragonsong,' said Dirk.

Acer, Tilia and Salix were backing away from the door.

'What's going on?' said Tilia, who had been too far away to hear Dirk's speech.

'He's using the manuman weapon to murder dragons,' said Betula.

'He wants to schmunch the Council,' said Buxus.

'That's not what I signed up for,' said Acer. 'I thought we were killing manumans.'

'You stupid Bark-backs,' snarled Vainclaw. 'Hold your ground.'

'I can't go to prison,' said Salix. 'I'm only nine hundred and twenty-five. I've got my whole life ahead of me.'

'Never mind prison,' replied Buxus. 'We'll be banished to the Inner Core for this.'

'It's his fault,' snarled Betula, looking at Vainclaw.

'He fablifised to us,' added Tilia.

The banging came again. 'I repeat, this is Officer

217

Balti Grunling, open the door in the name of the Dragnet. You are all under arrest. Do not try to use Dragonsong. We are equipped with ear mufflers.'

'Once they get through that door, we'll all be cuffed. There's no escapalading the Dragnet,' said Tilia.

'There's a back door,' said Buxus. 'Come on, bark sisters, let's go.'

Forgetting about Dirk, Betula and Buxus led the other three towards the door by the stage, but Vainclaw flew over them, blocking the way with his wings. Dirk noticed his right wing was half the size of his left, torn and frayed at the edge.

'Kinghorns, stop,' demanded Vainclaw, 'I command you to stop.'

'Get out of the way, boss,' said Betula.

'It's every dragon for herself,' added Acer.

'You are Kinghorns. I am your master,' said Vainclaw, but all five Tree Dragons were now approaching him, heads lowered, not in deference, but in preparation for attack.

Acer pounced, sinking her teeth into Vainclaw's leg. The others attacked, snapping and scratching and biting.

'Get off me,' growled Vainclaw.

'We'll release you when you get out of our way,'

replied Betula.

'Hurts doesn't it,' said Dirk, standing up, glad not to be on the receiving end for a change.

Vainclaw kicked and fought, smoke pouring out of his nose like he was on fire, but each time he forced one to let go another attached herself to his limbs. He turned to Dirk.

'This is just the beginning, Mr Dilly,' he said. 'The Kinghorns will unite and the war will begin and we will win, and if you don't join us you will die.'

With these final words, a great red flame burst from his mouth, scorching the Tree Dragons and forcing them to let go. Vainclaw turned and fled, followed closely by the five Tree Dragons.

'No, don't leave Callum again,' whined Callum, collapsing on to the floor and wailing like a wounded animal. Dirk walked over to the stage and reached a paw out to touch the silver case. No shock. The hour was up. The machine had reset itself. He grabbed the handle in his mouth and carried it up the aisle.

'Stay away from us, you monster,' said the principal fearfully.

'What have you done with my daughter?' demanded Mr Bigsby.

Dirk recognised him as the politician from the TV

interview he had watched. He placed the case by his feet. 'You work for the Ministry of Defence, don't you? I believe this belongs to you.'

Mr Bigsby took the case. 'The QC3000? How did this get here?'

'It's a long story. Now, your daughter . . .'

Dirk walked to the end of the hall and opened the door to the red carpet. For a moment no one moved, then Holly jumped from behind a photographer, smiling. Her leg was completely healed over.

'Did it work?' she asked.

'Like a dream,' he said. 'They bought it. How did you do that voice?'

'I got help,' she replied, and Dirk saw over her shoulder a man holding a wide-brimmed hat slip into a grey Mercedes with a white stripe, and drive away.

He stretched out a paw and shook Holly's hand. 'Good work, partner.'

'You too, partner,' she replied, beaming at him.

'Holly?' said Mr Bigsby.

'Dad,' she shouted, letting go of Dirk's paw and running into her father's arms. He lifted her up and kissed her on the cheek and Holly didn't even mind when his wife joined in the hug.

Humans were a funny species, thought Dirk. They

were responsible for lots of good things, like TV and orange squash and tinned baked beans, and lots of bad things, like guns and bombs and irritating polyphonic mobile phone rings. Watching Holly and her parents reunited in a tearful hug, Dirk thought that maybe family was one of the good things.

On the other side of the hall Petal's mother was clicking her fingers in front of her daughter's face, saying, 'Petal? Petal, darling? What's wrong with her?'

Principal Palmer was walking around the hall inspecting all of the stunned audience members. 'What's wrong with all of them?'

'Please don't worry,' said Dirk, picking up the microphone and switching it back on at the wall. 'I will explain everything in a minute.' His voice resounded through the hall and out into the car park. 'But first I think it's time for me to sing a little song. A-one, a-two, a-one, two, three, four . . .'

Chapter Twenty-Six

Lying beside Dirk, in the shadow of the Tree Dragon, with blood gushing from her leg, Holly had thought she was going to die and, as she drifted in and out of consciousness, she realised that if she went now, she would die without ever having known her father. They had drifted apart since her mother's death and she supposed, in the back of her mind, she always thought they would drift back together. Now, it was too late. With this thought she had fallen asleep.

Holly. Wake up.

Holly was awoken by Dirk's thoughts, speaking inside her head.

I'm thinking to you, like the councillors did. Stay

absolutely still and listen. Blending isn't the only dragon skill you have picked up. You skin has healed over during your sleep.

Holly reached down and touched her leg. It was covered in dry blood, but the cut had gone and it no longer hurt.

There isn't much time. The hour is almost up. Soon the machine will reset itself. You need to escape through the back door, see if you can get as far as the stage, then I'll draw their attention.

Dirk told her what to do once she was out of the building and Holly wriggled along the floor, stopping and blending every few seconds to avoid detection. Ever so gradually, keeping her movements small, she reached the stage.

'Don't you think your fellow Kinghorns deserve to know who they'll be murdering with this human weapon?' she heard Dirk say as she slipped through the backstage door and ran across the room, jumping over the instrument cases to reach the back door. She carefully avoided banging into the policeman standing outside the door. He was as still as a mannequin. She found another policeman with a loudhailer and carefully prized it out of his hand.

Dirk had told her to pretend to be the Dragnet,

coming to arrest the Kinghorns. He was banking on the cowardly Tree Dragons running away rather than facing arrest but, as she got nearer to the red carpet, she began to worry that they would recognise her voice. After all, it wasn't just Vainclaw and the Tree Dragons. Callum was in there too.

By the side of the building she saw a familiar figure, standing motionless and hatless in his long overcoat.

Ladbroke Blake.

She slapped him hard in the face.

'What the . . .' he began, instinctively grabbing her wrist.

'Shh.' She placed her fingers to his lips. 'It's me, Holly.'

'What's going on?' said Ladbroke. 'What was that music?'

'It's difficult to explain.'

'More dragon business?'

Holly nodded and handed him the loudhailer. 'I need a favour,' she said and told him what to say.

'Balti Grunling?' said Ladbroke disbelievingly. 'Funny sort of name.'

'Look who's talking,' replied Holly, leading him to the door.

Ladbroke wrapped his knuckles on the door and

made the announcement, as Holly had told him.

'This is Officer Balti Grunling of Dragnet. We have reason to believe there is illegal Kinghorn activity within this building. Come out with your claws down and your mouths shut.'

Both of them dived back into the crowd and froze in case the Kinghorns called their bluff and opened the door.

After the second announcement the door did eventually open, and Ladbroke saw the familiar figure of Dirk Dilly appear, so he slipped away, picking his hat up off the ground, noticing that two holes had been punched in the wide brim.

What has that dragon got against my hat? he wondered as he drove away.

Holly was relieved to see Dirk was OK, but there was someone she needed to see more. She found her dad and threw her arms around him. He picked her up and kissed her cheek.

'Dad,' she said. 'Are you all right?'

'I thought I'd lost you.'

'What's happening?' asked his wife. 'We thought that monster had killed you.'

'I'm all right,' she said to both of them. 'I've missed you.'

Dirk said something into the microphone.

'I miss you too,' said her dad.

His big-haired wife looked at Dirk and said, 'Is that thing your friend?'

'He's not a thing. He's a red-backed, green-bellied, urban-based Mountain Dragon and, yes, he's my friend.'

Mr Bigsby looked back at his daughter and said, 'You can come home if you want. We'll find a school near-by, a good one, one you don't have to run away from all the time.'

Dirk's voice filled the hall, saying, 'But first I think it's time for me to sing a little song.'

'I'd like that,' said Holly, tears in her eyes.

'A-one, a-two, a-one, two, three, four . . .'

Holly hugged her parents, and they all listened to the beautiful music which filled the air and entered their souls, the melodies and rhythms becoming part of them, like they were coming from within.

'Ow,' said Holly, holding her cheek. 'That really hurt.'

'I told you. It's the best way out of the trance.'

'I just think you could do it a little gentler when it's me, that's all.'

Holly looked at her dad and his wife, hugging each

other, a space between them where she had been.

'You're going to make them forget all this, aren't you?' she said.

'I'm sorry, Holly. I have to. You know what would happen.'

'Yes,' she said sadly. 'What now?'

'Everyone's back in the trance and it's my voice they've heard first this time,' said Dirk.

'Isn't there a danger they'll remember something?' asked Holly, thinking about her dad.

'They shouldn't but if they do get the occasional flashback, it'll seem so improbable that they'll think they're remembering some movie they've seen or a book they've read.'

She saw Callum crouching down by the stage, wearing the same faraway look in his eyes as everyone else. 'What about him?'

'I don't know,' said Dirk. 'For everyone else this is just one memory. It shouldn't be difficult to erase it, but Callum's had a long time living in fear. He's internalised the dragons that haunt him. Listen.' Dirk turned to the boy. 'Callum, there are no such things as dragons.'

'I know, they're in my head,' replied Callum. 'They're all in my head.'

Dirk turned back to Holly. 'Dragonsong is powerful

227

but one song can't undo all that torment. It seems that Vainclaw has been in communication with him since the kidnapping, grooming him to work for the Kinghorns.'

'But what if Vainclaw tries to use him again?'

'We can only hope he doesn't think it's worth the risk.'

Dirk held the microphone to his mouth and instructed Principal Palmer, Petal's mother, the Prime Minister, and Holly's dad and his wife to take their seats. They did so unquestioningly. He told Callum to take his place in the band with his French horn, and Petal to go backstage.

Then he addressed the front row, saying, 'When you awake none of you will remember anything about dragons. Dragons are no more than myths, stories to tell kids. Mr Bigsby, you will take the QC3000 back to the Ministry, saying you recovered it by chance and recommending a review into the security procedures which allowed something so important to go missing. Prime Minister Thackley, you will call an end to the AOG project. The world has enough natural disasters without adding our own.'

Holly whispered something in Dirk's ear and he addressed the entire audience. 'All any of you will remember when you wake up is that this was the best school concert ever. Every performance was brilliant, including a solo by Callum Thackley and a great number from Petal Moses. The band played beautifully and it was one of the best nights of your life.' Dirk switched off the microphone and said, 'Now, let's get rid of the evidence.'

Dirk found a mop backstage and cleaned up the pools of red and green blood, while Holly removed the film from the TV cameras and retrieved the Dragonsong CD from the stereo. She placed them all in a bin, which she handed to Dirk. He took a deep breath and burnt the lot to cinders.

When they had finished Holly asked, 'How are we going to wake them all up?'

'I've thought about this. Watch,' Dirk said, switching the microphone back on and saying, 'Now, could everyone stand up, raise your right hand and hold it in front of the person to your left's face. If you do not have anyone to your left, please hold it in front of the person behind you.'

The whole hall and everyone outside turned to face each other, hands outstretched. Holly did a quick scout to check that everyone was covered.

'Everyone got a slapping partner?' said Dirk.

'Just one left, but I can do that one,' said Holly, remembering Petal.

'As soon as I say this, I'm gone,' said Dirk.

Holly threw her arms around his soft green belly and hugged him tightly then followed him into the back-stage room, where he took the microphone to the door.

'Ready?' he said.

Holly lifted her hand level with Petal's face and nodded. 'Ready.'

'On the count of three,' Dirk said into the microphone, 'slap the person you're standing next to in the face.'

'One . . . two . . .'

'This is for Little Willow,' said Holly.

'Three.'

Holly slapped Petal hard in the face and ran back into the hall, jumping on stage to watch everyone coming out of their stupor.

For a stunned moment the audience stood staring at each other, rubbing their sore cheeks, then Principal Palmer began to clap. The Prime Minister joined in, followed by Petal's famous mother and Holly's dad and his wife. Soon, the whole hall was applauding. And not just inside the hall. The armed policeman with the face like a bulldog, Hamish the security guard, the showbiz reporter, everyone clapped like their lives depended on it. Holly saw Moji and grinned at her. All the people along the red carpet cheered and waved their auto-graph books in the air.

Looking surprisingly unfazed, Miss Gilfeather smiled and told the band to stand up and take a bow. Holly heard Sandy say to Julian, 'We must have been good. I don't even remember playing.'

All the parents came forward to congratulate their children and Holly found her dad, holding the silver case tightly in one hand.

'Well done, Holly,' he said. 'That was a magnificent performance.'

'Yes, we're both very proud,' said his big-haired wife.

For the second time that evening Holly hugged them both.

'It's quiet at home without you,' said her dad.

'Can I come home, then?' she replied.

He looked at his wife and sighed. 'You would have to promise to go to school and to behave. The Prime Minister says I have a good chance of making the Cabinet if we win the election.'

'I promise,' said Holly.

Mr Bigsby smiled. 'OK. I think there are a couple of

schools in the area you haven't tried.'

She thought she noticed a twinge of irritation cross his wife's face, but she didn't contradict him, so Holly smiled and said, 'I'd like that.'

She turned to see Callum, standing awkwardly in front of his dad.

'Well done, Callum,' said the Prime Minister.

'Thank you,' replied Callum, smoothing down his hair. 'I'm glad you enjoyed it. I like music. It takes you away.'

'Your nose is bleeding,' said his father.

Callum touched his nose and looked at the blood on his fingers. Holly tried to see in his eyes if he showed signs of remembering, but it was impossible to tell. Not that it mattered. He was harmless without the Kinghorns and they had gone now.

Everything was back to normal and she was going home.

Chapter Twenty-Seven

Dirk watched the smoke drift up from his nostrils into the sunbeams that shone through the blinds. It felt good to be back home and now that he had paid his rent with the cheque from Mrs Rosenfield, he was happily taking a few days off, relaxing behind his desk with a half-eaten tin of beans, a glass of orange squash on the rocks, and the TV remote within easy grabbing distance. Life didn't get any better than this.

The phone rang. Dirk tried to ignore it, but Mrs Klingerflim shouted, 'Your telephone is ringing, Mr Dilly . . . Mr Dilly . . .'

He flicked the receiver off the hook with his tail and caught it in his right paw.

'The Dragon Detective Agency. Dirk Dilly speaking,' he said.

'Oh, Mr Dilly, I'm so glad you're in. I wanted to thank you personally.'

'Hello, Mrs Rosenfield,' he replied, recognising the voice. 'I got your cheque. Is everything all right?'

'It's better than all right. I don't know what you did but, since he got back, my husband has been a changed man. He's attentive and sweet. He's talking about a second honeymoon. And he's finally given up all that dragon nonsense.'

'I'm glad to hear that,' said Dirk.

'He did say something about stamp collecting, but I suppose it's good to have interests outside work, isn't it?'

'I suppose it is,' said Dirk, instinctively going to stroke Willow, then remembering that Holly had collected her the previous day. Dirk was pleased that Holly was back in London. They would be able to see each other more often and she was happy to be back with her family and cat. Dirk had said good riddance to the dumb animal, but now she was gone the room felt oddly empty.

'He's giving all of his old books to a local charity shop this weekend,' continued Mrs Rosenfield. 'It's amazing. I'll certainly recommend you to anyone who needs a private detective in the future.'

'Please do that, Mrs Rosenfield. I'm glad you're happy.'

'Goodbye, Mr Dilly.'

'Goodbye, Mrs Rosenfield.' Dirk put down the phone.

It was nice to have a satisfied customer for a change. The problem with detective work was that even if you did a good job, your client discovered that, yes, her husband was having an affair, or no, their son didn't want to come back home, and so on. Happy endings were hard to come by in his line of work. He felt bad that it had taken Dragonsong to get a happy ending for the Rosenfields. He detested the misuse of Dragonsong. It was supposed to be a gift but, as he had said to Holly, lots of good dragons had been killed because of it.

Dirk watched the smoke trail take the form of a mountain lake and remembered the time he had found his mother's dead body. It was a human sword that had killed her, but there was never any doubt in Dirk's mind that Dragonsong had made her vulnerable.

No longer feeling relaxed, Dirk pushed open the window and took to the roofs of London, heading nowhere in particular, but making big daring jumps that took all his concentration, leaving no room for unhappy memories.

He hadn't been thinking where he was heading, so he was surprised when he found himself on a roof across the road from the Rosenfields' house. The front door opened and Professor Rosenfield exited the house, carrying a large cardboard box to his car.

'I won't be long, darling,' he called. 'I'll drop these off then pop to the supermarket to pick up something nice for dinner.'

Dirk followed the car to the local high street, where Rosenfield parked on double yellows, quickly got out, put the cardboard box outside a charity shop, and drove off again.

Dirk remained on top of the shoe shop opposite, wondering whether he had been right to rob the professor of his lifelong hobby. Not that humans ever got anything right about dragons. In all the books they had written, the pictures they had drawn and the films they had made on the subject, humans rarely happened across anything that was factually correct.

A young couple, walking side by side in silence, stopped by the charity shop and the young man began to rummage inside the cardboard box.

'You're not supposed to touch that,' snapped his girl-friend.

He pulled out a book.

'Put that back,' she said.

'They're only being thrown away,' he replied.

'No, they're being donated to charity,' she said. 'That's different.'

The man discarded the book and they carried on walking. 'It looked rubbish anyway. What did you want to talk to me about?' Dirk heard him ask.

'I don't want to go out with you any more. I've met someone else down the laundrette . . .' said the girl, as they disappeared down the road.

Dirk looked at the book lying on top of the cardboard box. It had a red cover and a white zigzagged line across the front. He recognised it at once but the high street was too busy to get it, so he winged his way home.

Late that night, when both hands on his old wall clock were facing up, Dirk pushed open the door to his office and crept into the hallway. Every stair creaked on the way down and he almost knocked a picture off with his tail, but he found the kitchen and switched on his torch. He pulled down the box of books from the high shelf and there it was, the same book with the red cover and the white zigzag across it. He opened it. The title was printed on the inside page.

DRAGONLORE
A Scientific Study of Dragons
By Ivor Klingerflim

He turned to the introduction.

There are many different types of dragon in the world, each with its own unique set of characteristics. A Sea Dragon, for example, has a grey back with a blue underbelly; whereas a Mountain Dragon's colours are red and green respectively. A Tree Dragon's skin resembles that of a tree bark, while a Desert Dragon at rest is easily mistaken for a cactus. All winged dragons have hard backs and soft bellies, although a Sea Dragon's back will soften after a sustained period underwater to facilitate swimming. Once out of the water, the Sea Dragon's back takes a few days to harden again, during which time it tends to hide in a waterside cave.

Dirk turned to another chapter and found more detailed descriptions, all illustrated with line drawings. Everything was spot on, saying where they could be found, what powers each type had, temperaments, diet. Everything. The last chapter speculated the reason for their disappearance, suggesting that they had probably gone into hiding around the Middle Ages.

The kitchen light came on.

'Oh, it's you, Mr Dilly. I thought we had burglars,' said Mrs Klingerflim, appearing behind him, wearing a pink nightie and brandishing a rusty fire poker. 'That's my dear Ivor's book. I'm particularly fond of chapter twelve, all about Sky Dragons, but then I suppose that's probably because I wrote most of it.'

Dirk handed the book to the old lady. 'Mrs Klingerflim?' he said.

'Yes, Mr Dilly?'

'You know I'm a dragon, don't you?'

She laughed. 'It's difficult not to notice, really, isn't it?' she replied. 'Shall we have a cup of tea? And biscuits. I've got some nice custard creams in a tin somewhere.'

By the same author

THE
DRAGON
DETECTIVE
AGENCY

Whatever your private detective needs, call
The Dragon Detective Agency for a quick,
reliable and flame retardant service.

BLOOMSBURY

www.bloomsbury.com